Bogs, Brews, and Banshees

Book One in
The Skye O'Shea Cozy Mysteries

Rowan Dillon

Green Dragon Publishing

Published 2024

Published by Green Dragon Publishing
Beacon Falls, CT
www.GreenDragonArtist.com

This book contains words and names from other languages, and the pronunciation of such words are different from English. I have included a Pronunciation Guide and Glossary in the back of this book for your guidance on these.

CHAPTER ONE

The plane jolted, and I clung to the armrests, my eyes squeezed shut. My heart was racing so fast, I thought it would burst out of my chest, and I ached to stand on solid ground. Any ground would do, even Miami, despite my haunted memories. This rough journey echoed the chapter I'd just closed.

Being in the sky seemed unnatural, despite my name being Skye.

A kind voice cut through the chaos. "Miss O'Shea, can I get you anything?"

I cracked open a reluctant eye, greeted by the concerned gaze of a flight attendant. With a shake of my head, I retreated into my cocoon of anxiety.

Odd music filtered into my panic. A haunting tune, unfamiliar yet strangely comforting. Along with that, a memory of my Gran's voice assured me. *Be calm,* mo chroí. *You will be safe.*

Her face floated in my memory as I last saw her, about twenty years ago. Her once-red hair had faded to pale peach streaked with white. She still had freckles like mine, but her wrinkles and age spots masked them. But she always had a smile for me.

I loved my Gran, though I hadn't visited her since I was a child. We'd written for years, sharing more of our lives and dreams than I had with anyone, even my soon-to-be-ex-husband, Armand. I would miss those letters so much. I had truly treasured each one. My throat choked with tears, but I swallowed them down.

After the turbulence eased, a weird sound made me peek out, just to see a young boy peering over the seat in front of me, making funny faces. He'd been doing this most of the flight and I was charmed. His hair had the same shade of chestnut brown as mine. I might not have had any children of my own, but I could appreciate a quiet child any day of the week.

Though I still felt queasy from the turbulence, I gave him a weak grin. That made him make even funnier faces, and I rewarded him with a heart-felt chuckle.

He disappeared from my view and I glanced out of the window. We must have been getting close to the airport, as the plane had descended below the clouds. The landscape below me was a quilt of odd-shaped farms in forty shades of green, something out of a story. The perfect manifestation of my idealized imagination.

While I'd always longed to return, first Mom had died, then I was in college, then I was married… and finances had never given me the chance, before now.

To keep my mind off the landing, I pulled out my puzzle book and started a new cryptic crossword. Losing myself in a puzzle was one of my favorite escapes.

As the transaltantic flight landed and the exhausted passengers shuffled off, I trudged through the arrivals section of the bustling airport, the weight of my recent past pressed heavily on me.

First, I found the bathroom. Airplanes have barely adequate facilities, especially for someone with, to put it politely, an ample backside. I brushed my shoulder-length hair and ignored the few gray strands, new arrivals since Armand left. At least my freckles made me seem younger.

The surrounding scene was one of ordinary airport chaos: children crying, weary travelers with suitcases that have seen better days, and announcement boards flickering with updates.

When I approached the baggage carousel, I stared at a tall, ornate grandfather clock stationed oddly near the exit from Terminal Two, all dark wood and antique decorations.

It wasn't the clock itself that was strange. Instead, the pendulum caught my curiosity. Rather than swinging back and forth in a consistent rhythm, it seemed to be dancing. Swaying left, then circling right, it paused, and dipped, all while emitting a soft, harmonious tune, like the one on the plane. A melody both familiar and utterly alien.

I rubbed my eyes, attributing the illusion to my exhaustion. Then a faint, silvery glow surrounded the clock, and people walking through that glow slowed, as if walking through

Jell-O. Their voices grew distorted, like they were submerged under water.

As I glanced around to see if anyone else noticed the phenomenon, travelers pushed past me, seemingly oblivious to the clock and its magical aura.

A small, elderly woman with glittering black eyes and a scarf of bright green and blue appeared beside me, looking like someone out of a fairy tale. She seemed half-familiar, almost similar to my Gran. That couldn't be, could it? Gran had died. She didn't have any close relatives, otherwise they would have inherited things.

The woman whispered, "Not everyone sees the dance of time, dearie. Consider yourself chosen."

Before I could respond, I glimpsed my purple suitcase on the carousel, and my attention snapped away. When I turned back, the old woman was gone, and the clock's pendulum was swinging normally.

I scrubbed at my face. I must be more exhausted than I thought, falling asleep while just waiting for my baggage. I clenched my fists and legs as I bent to pluck my suitcase from the conveyor belt, trying to stimulate my circulation and get some energy back.

Once I got my luggage, a woman using a walker was in my way, and I waited as she glared at me, then shuffled by. She reminded me of the strange woman I'd seen at a job interview in Miami. That had been the same day I'd learned about Gran's death, and a shiver ran down my spine. Were they the same person? How could that be? *Get a hold of yourself, Skye.* I shook off the notion as impossible.

Scanning the crowds, I searched for my ride. There, a youngish man with pale skin and red hair clutched a sign with my name on it. Of course, he had red hair. I'd always wished for straight, red hair like my Gran, but mine was a disappointing chestnut brown and hopelessly wavy.

As I approached the man with the sign, he asked, "Mrs. O'Shea?"

I wrestled my bag into place as I swallowed back an angry retort. I should be used to correcting people by now. "Miss O'Shea, please. I had another name when I was married."

A flicker of judgment passed over his expression as he helped me with my luggage. but I didn't care. Getting divorced was the best thing that ever happened to me. Well, would happen, as it wasn't final yet. Between my rotten ex-husband and my grandmother's death, my life had been filled with lawyers this year.

It had taken months of paperwork, phone calls, packing, and not a few tears of frustration and melancholy, but I was finally in Ireland. I had to sell off almost everything I owned–car, furniture, books, anything I had of value, just to keep myself afloat until the will was settled.

"I'm Niall, and I can take you to Mr. Curran's office. My car's this way."

I'm glad the lawyer, or solicitor, or whatever they were called here, had sent a driver. I couldn't even imagine me jumping into a rental car and tooling down the highway on the wrong side of the road, fresh from a ten-hour flight. I used to be a hard-as-nails nurse, but now I cried at commercials. I was a mess in so many ways.

As we walked outside, I breathed in the fresh air with delight. May was brutal in Miami with violent rainstorms every afternoon. High humidity made it worse. Here in Ireland, it was a lovely 70 degrees, even in the direct sunlight. And yes, it was humid, but not nearly as bad as Miami in the summer.

We were silent as Niall drove into Dublin. Rubbernecking like the rankest tourist, I tried to see everything, comparing each street to those in Miami, watching people stroll down the busy sidewalk, the random ancient buildings nestled amongst the modern ones.

My driver glanced at me as he turned a corner onto a narrow, one-way street. "First time in Ireland?"

"No, I came as a child. This is my first time in Dublin."

So many things seemed strange. Street signs on the sides of buildings in both English and Irish. Rows of connected houses, all identical except for brightly painted doors. Actual cobblestones on some of the alleys we passed. Traditional pubs perched on each corner, with names like *O'Donovan's* or *Murphy's*. Gift shops filled with tourist tat, all sparkling shamrocks and stuffed sheep.

And yet, crowds of pedestrians filled the sidewalks, all hurrying somewhere, just like any big city.

We pulled into a narrow alley and then a hidden parking lot, big enough for perhaps six cars. Still silent, we went inside and took an elevator into a rather simple office. No glitzy glass and chrome here–just cream-colored walls, dark wooden desks, and a few potted plants. Like something out of the 80s.

Niall said, "If you'd just wait here, Miss O'Shea, I'll fetch Mr. Curran."

So, I perched on the edge of the sage green sofa and tried not to stare at the receptionist. She also had red hair. Jeez, did everyone here have red hair?

Glancing at the magazines on the table, I noted their titles. *In Dublin. Ireland's Own. House and Home.* None were recent editions, of course. At least *that* was the same as Miami. I was just about to grab one when a portly dark-haired man emerged. "Mrs. O'Shea?"

"I go by Miss O'Shea, now. I dropped the Mrs. a while ago, when I took back my maiden name."

"Ah yes, of course. Please, come into my office. We have many things to finish this morning."

He wasn't kidding. We shuffled through a thick pile of papers, signing and dating and initialing and he brought his receptionist in to witness half of them.

Gran Saoirse's house and B&B in Ballybás, County Cork. The attached pub, O'Shea's. Tears began to choke my breath again, wishing I'd been there for Gran's last days. I still didn't understand why she wouldn't have told me. I would have dropped everything to be there with her. Not that I had much of everything left at that point.

Staring at the words, my heart skipped a beat. "Five acres? Gran had five acres?" I didn't have a good grasp of acres. That was a lot, wasn't it? Certainly, a great deal more than a 500-square-foot apartment in a sketchy neighborhood of Miami.

"Yes, Miss O'Shea. Five acres of woods and farm, a house, with an attached pub. Some of the bedrooms were kitted out as B&B rooms."

I only remembered a few images from staying with her as a child. A big house with colorful rooms and lots of books. I didn't remember the pub, though.

Finally, after the last paper was signed, he handed me a set of keys. I stared at them as if they were a venomous snake. "What are these?"

"Keys to your pub, home, and car, Miss O'Shea. Your grandmother had us bring her vehicle here when she realized she was dying."

I swallowed away more sudden tears as I took the cool bits of metal, grasping them tight in my fingers. So tight, they were cutting into my palm. They helped reduce a wave of dizziness. "Where…where is it parked?"

Mr. Curran rose and opened the door. "I'll bring you down there. You'll be happy to know it's an automatic transmission."

I hadn't even considered that it would be a manual. I could drive one, but it had been many years since I had. Following him back down to the street, we stopped next to a tiny sky-blue car.

The back logo said Suzuki Splash. I'd never even heard of that model. Perhaps it aspired to be a car someday. When it grew up.

Mr. Curran handed me a piece of paper. "Here is the address of your new place. Please let me know if there's anything else I can do to help you settle in."

Anything else? I had a million questions bubbling up inside me. None of them would rise from the fray to emerge from my mouth. Asking questions of lawyers was always expensive. Or solicitors. I gave him a weak smile, thanked him for all his help, and shook his hand. He helped me get my luggage into the trunk of the car, and waved as he walked back to his office.

Once he disappeared, I stared at the car. Would I even fit in the seat? I'd never driven on the left. I was rather tall for a woman and had never been thin. Even being on my feet for twelve-hour shifts as a nurse hadn't melted off the pounds.

With a sigh, I opened the door. Well, I tried. The car was still locked. I chuckled at my idiocy, unlocked it, and got inside. I fit well enough, but I wouldn't want to do a cross-country trip in it.

And then I realized I'd opened the wrong side. The driver's seat was on the right side in Irish vehicles, and I'd have to learn to drive on the left. I walked to the other side and unlocked it, getting in again.

I sat with my hands on the wheel, trying to get used to being on the right side of the car. And trying to stave off panic. Had I just done this? Changed my entire life in a few months?

I glanced outside, watching corporate types walking down the sidewalk, intent on their singular missions. Something flickered in the corner of my vision, but when I looked, nothing was there. Just a random flash of light off something, perhaps.

This massive change hadn't been my idea. I'd been mostly happy working as a nurse, and content being married. However, my best friend and my husband had other ideas. My boss at work had been slime, getting me framed for a mistake I hadn't made. So, when this opportunity came, I grabbed it.

I'd never been the mad one, the one who was willing to just jump ship into an entirely new adventure. This time, I did it, and I was still screaming in the back of my mind that this was all a mistake, that I'd fail horribly.

But here I was, in my new almost-car, listening to Dublin traffic drive by, and mustering up the courage to embark on a new life.

I took a deep breath, twisted the key, and turned on my blinker. Time to change lanes.

Despite the lovely gift of an almost-car, I had no intention of driving it all the way to Cork that day. I'd been traveling since 7 pm the night before, in Miami. I tried to count how many hours I'd been awake now, but my mind refused to work properly.

The flight was two hours to Newark, a two-hour layover, then another seven to Dublin. That was eleven so far. I'd arrived at eleven in the morning, then spent another two hours with the lawyer.

Thirteen hours? It seemed like longer. Oh, right, of course, I'd spent the day before cleaning my apartment, dropping off the keys to the landlord, all that stuff. Plus losing five hours changing time zones.

I'd been awake for twelve hours before I started traveling. Ugh, that meant I'd been awake for twenty-five hours, and I was about ready to drop dead on my feet.

Well, I'd better get to my hotel. I had reserved a room near Heuston Station, thinking I'd have to take a train to Cork. Sure, I had a car now, but I still needed the room. In fact, I was beginning to seriously droop.

I drove slowly through the streets of Dublin. It was packed with midday traffic anyhow, so no one was going fast, but I was glad of it. I wouldn't want to be zipping through these narrow, crowded streets, especially in this weird car.

I found Tipperary House Hotel and narrowed my eyes at the very budget façade. But this was only for one night, and I wasn't exactly swimming in cash. This would have to do.

After parking in the nearby lot, I dragged myself and my overnight bag into the lobby, checked in, and shuffled up to my room. All of that was a daze. Despite it being barely two, I fell onto the bed and slept without even taking my clothes off.

I woke to music playing, an ethereal tune I almost recognized. *Time to wake up!*

I jumped up, not knowing where I was or how I got there, and the music disappeared.

I'd always heard bits of music in my head. However, I'd also long since learned not to mention it to anyone. Same with seeing colors on people. My weird brain often played tricks on me.

The room was completely unfamiliar, with one dark blue accent wall and a wooden backboard, and my heart began to race. Then memories started clicking into place, and I stared out my window onto the street. I was actually in Dublin. I felt silly repeating that to myself so often, but I still wasn't used to the idea.

I must have slept a good five hours, and my stomach was rumbling. After I scrubbed my face and brushed my hair, I felt marginally less exhausted. I'd had nothing for lunch, and my stomach was demanding to be fed. Still, I had no wish to navigate city traffic again, especially near rush hour, so I descended to the lobby, searching for meal options.

Approaching the front desk clerk, I asked, "Do you have a restaurant in-house?"

The younger woman cocked her head. "No, we've nothing inside. There're plenty of choices just on this street. The Chesterfield and the Iveagh are in the Aisling Hotel next door on the right. Either are delightful for a splurge. If you're looking for something a bit more affordable, there's a half dozen places about two streets down. There's a grand chippie, a sandwich shop, and an Italian take-away, as well as more posh restaurants."

"A chippie?"

She let out a chuckle. "A fish and chips place."

Fish and chips sounded like exactly what I wanted for my first meal in Ireland. I thanked her and stepped outside, breathing in the city air. Sure, that sounded odd. But I grew up in the city. I knew the smells and they were a comfort, even if they were obnoxious. The quiet of the countryside could be downright unsettling for a city girl.

Peering in each direction, I turned to the right, passed the Aisling Hotel, and kept walking. Just when I'd decided that *two streets* was a gross exaggeration, I found the area she described. A pub, a coffee place, and a few other shops.

While I wanted that fish and chips, I didn't know if my exhausted legs would make the trip much further and still make it back to the hotel. Which sounded ridiculous, because I was thirty, not seventy, but it had been a very, very long day.

So, I chose the first place, a pub called Duggans. As soon as I walked in, I smelt pizza, and had to admit, I was a bit disappointed. Pizza, in Ireland? That didn't sound right. Still, I hadn't been here in years, and only had vague memories of it. Besides, I hadn't been going to pubs at that age.

Intellectually, I knew they'd have just as much of a variety of foods as we did in America, or at least close. For now, I wanted the traditional meals to satisfy my inner tourist.

Speaking of tourists, the décor was spot on to what I expected. Dark wood, a gleaming bar, pictures of Olde Ireland on the walls. Was Gran's pub looked like this? I didn't remember her having a pub when I had been here, but maybe they just didn't show me that part of the building.

As I grabbed a seat, I stared at the menu. Yup, pizza and wings and burgers. Then my eyes found a listing for all-day breakfast, and a smile crept across my face. I used to love the full fry-up Granny Saoirse would make when I visited. Eggs, sausage, rasher bacon, black pudding, mushrooms, tomato, and homemade brown bread.

She used to give me a warm smile as she placed the full plate in front of me. "This'll keep you going through anything, *mo chroí*. Just you eat that all up, and you'll be set for the day."

I always got a warm feeling when she called me *mo chroí*. It meant *my heart*, and I couldn't think of a lovelier term.

Shaking off the nostalgia, I glanced around, wondering if a server would come and get my order. Then I remembered that Granny wrote about pub etiquette. At a pub, I'm supposed to order at the bar. So, feeling horribly self-conscious, I bellied up to the bar and waited for the barman to notice me.

To be fair, he did so quickly, nodding to the menu in my hand. "Aye, luv. What'll you have?"

"A full Irish breakfast, please?"

"Ah, American, are ye? Will you want everything with that? Toast and beans and black pudding?"

I grinned. "Absolutely."

He wrote on his pad and nodded. "And what'll ye be drinking?"

I hadn't even considered that. I was at a bar, I wasn't driving, and I could enjoy my first pint in Ireland. "A pint of Guinness, please."

I'd never had it, but I needed to try the 'black stuff,' if I was going to make a go of running a pub in Ireland, didn't I?

If I could.

CHAPTER TWO

After the enormous meal, my still-fatigued body insisted on more rest. I trudged back to my hotel and, despite the earlier nap and the fact that it was barely eight o'clock, I collapsed and slept like the dead.

Luckily, when I finally woke twelve hours later, I felt fresh as a daisy and ready to wrestle alligators. Well, maybe a large iguana. Okay, fine, a gecko, then.

After an easy check out and a panicked moment when I forgot what my car looked like, I stuffed my luggage back into the sky-blue almost-car and pulled out of the garage, out of Dublin, and onto the highway.

Maybe I should give this car a name? I never gave my car in Miami a name. It had always been on the edge of dying, so I didn't want to risk losing it after naming it. This car needed one. The Shamrocklet? Pale Pixie? The Blue Buggy? The Sky-Blue Bantam? I'd have to think about that for a while.

The drive was supposed to take me about four hours. As the trees were tall on either side of the M7 motorway, I didn't get to see much of the countryside. Occasionally, I got glimpses of rolling green hills, sheep farms, or towns clumped on either side of the road, but mostly trees.

I was fine with trees, as it was a darn sight better than the flat nothing surrounding Florida highways.

The road veered south and followed along the coast for a few miles. Occasionally, I caught a hint of sound, the sparkling waves of the sea playing a gentle melody, harmonizing with the distant bleat of sheep. I had no idea if I could hear it while driving, or if it was my overactive imagination.

I'd been tooling down the highway for about an hour, lost in my thoughts, when an enormous tower came into sight. An actual castle, right next to the road! I simply had to stop to explore. As I slammed on my brakes to pull into the long driveway, two people behind me honked, and I waved sorry as they went by. One angry lout kept honking and shook his fist at me.

I didn't care. *An actual castle!* I drove down the one-lane driveway slowly, almost clipping the corner of a wooden post fence. No one was around. I remembered Gran wrote about something called the pedestrian's right of way. That, as long as you weren't damaging anything, you could walk through private land. Still, I didn't know if that applied to everyone.

A red car was already parked in the lot, and I took a spot three down. Feeling incredibly conspicuous, I climbed out of the car and stared up at the mossy round stone tower. Then I whipped out my phone and took at least twenty photos from different angles and perspectives. Almost as if I was a real photographer.

Every nook and corner seemed to hum with stories, from the ancient oaks lining the narrow roads to the faint scent of turf fires wafting through the air. Then clouds blotted out the sun and everything turned dim.

A sense of mystery hung shrouded around the tower, urging me to discover its secrets. How could I do that from outside? I circled the tower, searching for a way in.

The door had an enormous, rusted iron latch and a padlock. I was both disappointed that I wouldn't be able to explore and relieved that I wouldn't have to decide if I was brave enough to enter. I touched the rough, rusty metal, cold beneath my hands. A lock on the past, forcing me to go into the future.

Then, a bee buzzed around me and landed right on the lock. I'd always loved anything to do with bees. I'd had to leave behind my bee bookmarks, bee t-shirts, even a stuffed bee toy. They were supposed to be a symbol of abundance and kindness.

I guess the lock was telling me to look forward, and the bee was telling me my future would be abundant. After a few moments of soaking in the random dose of historic wonder, I turned around.

Angry voices filtered through my reverie. Cautiously, I peeked around the tower's corner, and spied two men and a woman. The larger man had wide shoulders and clenched fists.

Standing next to him was a young man wearing aqua scrubs, slightly built with flyaway blond hair. This second man was glaring at a thin woman about the same age, with black hair and wearing a blindingly pink sundress.

The woman sounded petulant. "But I don't want to go to Dublin, Gerald! I want to go back!"

They were between me and the car park, so I'd have to pass them to escape. While I was pondering what other options I had, the woman glanced up and pursed her lips. "Brian, there's someone over there."

The larger of the two men scowled at me. "Are you eavesdropping on us?"

"No, of course not! I was just leaving."

"What do you want?"

I stepped out from behind the tower wall, my hands up in surrender. "Nothing, I swear! Don't mind me."

Full of self-consciousness, every step felt awkward as I went by them and to the car park. All three glared me in silence.

Just as I got into my car, the thinner man said, "I still think we should go back to Dublin."

I wondered if they'd witnessed me taking all those silly photos, but then shrugged. They obviously had more on their mind than a random American tourist. I pulled back onto the road with a sigh.

As a child, I'd always dreamed of living in a castle. Not like a princess, with pretty dresses and fairy magic, but like a powerful queen, a mistress of my domain, in charge of all I surveyed.

Of course, a nurse in Miami didn't have the proper lineage to become a queen, unless I'd gotten lucky and snagged a prince to marry, like Grace Kelly or Meghan Markle. Instead, I'd snagged Armand, who had turned out to be the worst sort of toad.

My lovely mood dissolved into bitterness, and I gripped the steering wheel so tight, my fingers ached.

I needed to find my calm before I kept going. Pulling over to one side, I spent at least twenty minutes just staring across the countryside. Rolling hills. Two farmhouses, one with a crumbling shed. A few cows mooed at me. Breathing in and out, I finally felt ready to drive again.

The rest of the trip passed with only a few glances at the gorgeous scenery as I stewed in memories of Armand's betrayal and his subsequent cruelties. I replayed in my head every single time he played a nasty practical joke, or I discovered some new manipulation, engineered to make my life worse. His screaming fits in my face, his slamming on the brakes in traffic when we argued. Then my bitterness turned to my best friend, Marie, and her fresh treachery.

My teeth ached from clenching them too hard.

By the time I approached Ballybás, the place where my grandmother had lived most of her life, I was a seething pit of resentment.

Trying to put that away, at least for a little while, I drew in a deep, shuddering breath. Taking in the surroundings, I was struck by its charm. The world shifted ever so subtly to unveil a landscape untouched by time.

Whitewashed cottages with thatched roofs punctuated lush, rolling green hills. A circle of five standing stones perched on top of one hill, glittering in the sunlight. Each stood as a silent sentinel to myriad tales whispered through the ages. A hint of a rainbow surrounded them. I thought it was too sunny for a rainbow, but hey, this was Ireland. If rainbows wanted to dance in the sunshine, who was I to say no?

Here, in this charming village of a thousand souls, the frenzied pace of the modern world faded, replaced by the timeless rhythm of nature and community.

I slowed as I drove down the main street, drinking in the details. There was the corner store, just as Gran had described. The Garda office with the doctor's clinic next door. Gran had mentioned the local policeman and the physician were a married couple.

A large, glitzy pub loomed, but it couldn't be Gran's. Hers would be shuttered and dark. This one was open and freshly painted, with the name *O'Leary's* in bright red over the windows.

I glimpsed an art gallery, a gift shop filled with plastic shamrocks and stuffed sheep toys, and a café called The Blarney Scone. I giggled at the pun. The church steeple rose above it all.

My reverie was shattered by a horrid lurch and a loud crunch. I slammed on my brakes and the Sky-Blue Bantam screeched to a halt. "Holy sheep nuggets! What was that?"

I slammed the gear into park and struggled to shove the door open. Grunting and pushing, it wouldn't budge. When it finally sprang loose, I staggered out, trying to see what had happened.

To my left stood a car with a shattered front headlight. I peered at the new almost-car my Gran had given me and, sure enough, a matching shattered taillight stared back. My blood began to rise. This was a brand-new car! Well, new to me. Certainly, in better shape than any car I'd ever owned.

A man jumped out of the other car, his face red and contorted. I recognized him instantly from the castle. His face looked like a Florida thunderstorm. "Watch where you're going, woman!"

Adrenaline and anger rushed through my veins, and I lost any hold I had on my temper. "Me? You hit my car! Learn to drive, creep!"

The man strode right up to me, stopping inches from my face. I could feel the heat radiating from his flushed skin. "You think you can just waltz into this village and act like you own the place?"

My fright melded into anger, and his attitude made me reckless. I'd promised myself to never again cower from bullies and tried to channel Gran. "You don't know anything about me! Maybe I *do* own the place!"

The passenger door of his car creaked open, and the young woman dressed in bright pink emerged. She got between us, facing him. "Brian! She's right. She wasn't at fault."

Brian loomed over her, anger still oozing from his body language. He almost looked as if someone had painted him with a watercolor wash of red.

The third man, with the wispy hair, sat the back seat with a wary expression. "Cherie! Come here to me in the car. It's nothing to do with you."

Cherie raised her hands. "Patience Gerald! Alright, now, Brian, give over. And you, too. Let's just all calm down."

I locked gazes with Brian and clenched my teeth. I should back down, but I didn't want to. I'd done enough backing down with Armand. I'd promised myself I'd be different in this new place, with this new life. I was determined to stand up for myself more and not allow myself to be a doormat for anyone. Especially an angry jerk who acted like my ex-husband.

Still, it made sense to de-escalate. Forcing myself to stay calm, my voice was almost light-hearted. "You remind me of someone I once knew."

His brow furrowed, and he'd obviously not expected that tack. "Oh? And who's that, luv?"

The woman tried again, a hand on his chest. "Brian, please. Just leave her alone."

He growled at her, shoving her hand away. "Clear off, Cherie! This is exactly none of your business!"

For a moment, I felt certain he was going to strike her. Everyone froze for one horrific moment. Cherie grew pale as she backed away.

This must have satisfied Brian, as he turned back to me, his scowl growing to epic proportions. The young man from the car climbed out and grabbed Cherie's arm. After a few tense words with her, speaking in a tone too low for me to hear, they ran off together down a side street.

That left me alone with an angry man in my face. My temporary courage and ferocity drained away in an instant. I wanted to run away with them. Away to safety and anonymity.

Two other people rushed up to the scene from around a corner. An attractive dark-skinned woman about my age, who seemed to glow in a vivid green outfit, and a somewhat disheveled man with long, ash-blond hair in a ponytail, wearing flannel and jeans.

The woman glanced between Brian and me. The woman glanced between Brian and me. She spoke with a heavy Cork accent, but the few times I spoke to Gran on the phone made that easier for me to understand. "What was that crash? Is anyone hurt? I'm a doctor, Adanna McCarthy."

I shook my head, glaring at the blue car and its crunched-in taillight. "I'm fine, just a bit shaken. My car, however, is going to need some emergency care, I'm afraid."

The flannel-clad man crouched next to it, clicking with his tongue. I judged him to be in his late twenties. The doctor seemed younger. "It's not so bad. I'll leg it over to Ciaran's and he can fix that in less than an hour, like."

Meanwhile, the doctor questioned Brian. "What's your name? Did you lose consciousness?"

He glared at her with his arms straight at his side, as if he was suppressing the urge to shove her aside. More people gathered in the street, and suddenly I felt horribly self-conscious. This was *not* how I wanted to meet all my new neighbors, not by a long chalk.

Doctor McCarthy pulled me aside, her pretty face full of kind concern. "Are you sure you're not hurt? Did you hit your head? Does your neck ache?"

"No, nothing. It was just a fender bender."

"Are you staying in town? What's your name?"

"S-Skye. Skye O'Shea."

Her dark eyes grew wide as she grinned. "Ah, you're Saoirse's granddaughter, you must be. You have her eyes. Speaking of eyes, I still need to assess you. Can you look into mine?"

I tried to stare without blinking, still in a bit of a daze. "I know the drill. I'm a nurse. Really, I'll be fine."

She gave me a scowl. "That's as may be, but I still need to form my opinion. Did you hit your head?"

Her Cork accent was thick, but I remember Gran's was similar. I shook my head, but she said, "Please answer me verbally." "No, I didn't hit my head."

The doctor asked several other questions, asking about any pain in my neck, if I was dizzy, or if I had difficulty breathing.

Finally, she put her hands on her hips. "Well, your eyes are a bit glassy, but I think you'll do. Let's get you out of the spotlight. Saoirse's place is down this road."

The doctor turned to the ash-blond guy. "Seán! Can you take care of her car? I'm taking her for a calming drink. And let Dónal know about this?"

He stood and gave a nod. "Sure and I can do that, Adanna. A drink will soothe the nerves. Skye, will you trust me with your keys? I can take it direct to the garage."

I glanced back and forth between Adanna and Seán. "Who's Dónal?"

As I pulled the car key off my ring and placed it in his hand, Seán gave me a saucy grin. "He's the local Gard. He'll probably come by to ask some questions." All I could think about was that Seán had very blue eyes. Very unlike Armand's deep brown ones.

"Hey!" Brian growled, "What about my car?"

Sean turned to the older man. "I'm sure you're more than capable of fixing the damage from the accident you yourself caused, you eejit. After all, we reap what we sow, don't we?"

While Brian huffed and puffed, Doctor Adanna scowled at him, then spoke to Seán. "Make sure to get his insurance information, too. He could vanish tomorrow. He looks like that sort."

I didn't like someone else taking control of the situation. That seemed at odds with my determination to be in charge of my life.

But the doctor had a point, and I was still very rattled. Adrenaline drained away and my legs got shaky. "Fine. But only if *he,*" and I waved a hand toward Brian, "pays for the damages."

The angry man snarled, his face full of fury. A simmering shadow of red seemed to shroud him.

CHAPTER THREE

Doctor Adanna led me down one side street and to a building tucked away, lonely and dark. "This is Saoirse's place. Have you been here before, then?"

It had boards nailed over most of the muillioned windows on the ground floor, but one had fallen off. The name painted above them read *O'Shea's,* and a shudder ran through me. My name, on a pub. My surreal life just kicked up a notch.

"Only as a child, long ago." This was where Gran had lived, loved, and then died. Now it was mine. She'd gifted me more than a pub. She'd given me a new lease on life. Sure, it sounded corny, but it was utterly true. I sniffed back tears.

"Do you have keys? If not, I can leg it home to get my set, like."

"You have keys to my Gran's place?"

She let out a chuckle. "Only temporarily. She entrusted a set with my husband. He's been keeping them until you came.

Saoirse told me you'd arrive soon enough, and wise folks don't ignore her predictions. Do I need to go get the keys?"

"Uh, no. I've got mine here." I stared at the key ring. Mr. Curran had given me about a half dozen keys, but I had no idea which one worked for the pub.

Adanna held out her hand. "May I?"

My brain felt fuzzy. Maybe I was in shock, at least a little. I handed them over without a word. She tried two keys before finding the one that worked.

She swung the door open, and it creaked like something out of a horror movie. We exchanged a solemn glance, then she giggled. I couldn't help but chuckle in response. That broke the ice a bit.

"Come on in, then, and I'll get you set up. I know where the tea things are, and where I can get a dollop of something stronger."

As we stepped inside, dust tickled my nose and I let out an enormous sneeze.

The doctor said, "Bless you."

I needed all the blessings I could get, so I gave the doctor a grateful nod.

The scent of stale beer and old sweat hit me in the face. I would have to air this out for a year to get rid of all that. The dim interior was only lit by a few sunbeams shooting through the gap in the boards.

But Adanna didn't stop in the bar. She led me through one thick mahogany door and into a suite of rooms. These smelled much better, like lavender and peat smoke. A fireplace took up most of the south wall, while books covered the opposite one.

That made me grin, as Gran had loved to read as much as I did. Some were puzzle books, with crosswords and such, and I smiled even more. I was more like Gran than I'd realized. The rest of the room was homey and cozy, with a settee, a sideboard, several rugs and side tables. No television, though.

"Sit here, then. I'll fetch the tea."

The doctor gestured toward a comfortable-looking lounge chair covered in maroon velveteen, the arms and back rubbed thin. The sheer comfort of the chair called to me.

As I sunk in, I let out a sigh. This felt like home. I hadn't been here since I was a child, but all the memories were clicking into place. I half-expected Gran to come out of the kitchen with a tray of fresh-baked brown bread.

Adanna was clinking teacups in the kitchen, then the water was running. "I'll make a full pot, as Seán is sure to come back when he's done at the garage. Do you like a particular brand of tea? Saoirse has Barry's, but she's got a few of those herbal things, too."

"Barry's is fine. Thank you."

I didn't want her to be serving me, not in what was now my house, but it also felt rather nice. No one had ever catered to me before. Certainly not Armand; he expected me to care for him, even when I was working sixty hours a week and he lazed about.

The doctor returned, carrying a tray with cups, spoons, and a sugar bowl. "No milk, sorry. There isn't much left in the cupboard. Folks came by with meals for your gran before she died. She didn't have the strength to prepare anything herself, I'm afraid."

"Were you good friends with her?"

She sat on the settee, opposite me. "Fair enough, I'd say. She was always ready for a chat, and I do like a bit of the gossip. When the pub was open, we'd talk for hours over a pint. Then she started fading, and closed the pub. I came as much as I could, but as the only doctor in town, I came more on official business than as friends."

A twinge of betrayal hit, that I hadn't been given a chance to be there. Despite the fact that I had no choice in the matter, I didn't think I'd ever forgive myself for not being with her. "I'm glad she had friends nearby. Gran didn't even tell me she was ill, or I would have come sooner."

Adanna waved her hand. "That's exactly how she wanted things. She had no wish for your last memory of her to be a poor, sick old woman. Those are her direct words, mind you."

My twinge subsided. Gran always had planned things to her satisfaction. Luckily, her plans suited my own.

The kettle rumbled and popped, and Adanna went back into the kitchen. In her absence, I glanced around, trying to fit the room with my childhood memories. It seemed the same, for the most part, but a few details were different.

A movement in the corner caught my eye, and I squinted to see what it was. Then a huge black cat darted out of the corner and straight into the kitchen. The doctor let out a yelp. "Faelan! Behave yourself. I fed you this morning, you greedy guts. You'll get nothing until tonight, and you know that well!"

She came in with the teapot and two cups. "Now, let that brew, mind you. I know you Americans have some odd notions about tea."

I let out a chuckle. "Ah, don't worry. Gran taught me the proper ways."

"I would expect nothing less of her."

As we settled into a comfortable silence, I glanced back toward the door. "So, Gran has… uh, had a cat?"

"Sure, Faelan is his name. Huge black tomcat, he is. A great comfort to her in the last months, I can tell you. And a right devil the rest of the time, so."

"He lives inside, or outside, or both?"

Adanna cocked her head. "Both. He comes and goes as he pleases."

I glanced around at the tchotchkes and decorations. My gaze fell on a photograph of a large group of people in the pub. Picking up my now-brewed tea, I rose to examine it closer, and Adanna followed me.

Pointing each person out, she said, "Now, there's your Gran, and me next to her. Then my husband, Dónal. As Seán mentioned, he's the Gard. Our families have lived in this town for about five generations. Next to Dónal is Seán, you've met him.

He runs the beehives, as well as a general handyman business. He was born here, but his parents came from Cork City proper. A nice man, dependable and solid."

"Oh, right. I remember him." I also remembered Seán's lovely eyes. She gave me a sidelong glance, but I kept my expression neutral. This was a small town and I didn't want to feed the rumor mill so quickly. Besides, I was far from ready for a new relationship.

I pointed to the next person, wearing a priest's vestments with the white collar. "What's the priest's name?"

The doctor gave a quick nod. "That'll be Father Fraser. He's a wee bit shy, but he's from Scotland, so he's a recent blow-in."

"When did he move here?"

"Oh, near to ten years ago now. Said he had some sort of vision, so he asked his bishop to send him here."

Ten years. It would be a long time until I was accepted as a local, then. An actual vision? The doctor said it as if this was an everyday statement, not something out of a fantasy movie. Definitely a bit suspicious, especially from a woman of science.

Adanna pointed to an older man. "That's Padraig. He's a sheep farmer, but you'll never understand a word he says. No one does. He mumbles on about the Banshees, *Sluagh Sídhe, Fear Dearg*, and the fairies, much as anyone can tell."

I let out a chuckle and took a sip of my tea. Gran had told me about him in her letters. In fact, she'd mentioned many of these folks. Not so much about the Fear Dearg, whatever they might be, but about the people themselves.

The doctor gave a casual shrug. "But then again, maybe Padraig's got the right of it. You *do* hear the odd howl in the dark of the night."

The wind was fierce on the coast. Surely, that's all she meant. But her comment about the vision made me wonder.

Just as Adanna had pointed to the next person, a young woman with a wealth of wavy, honey-blond hair, there was a knock at the door. My head was already beginning to swim with new names and faces. I was never good at such things. Maybe because, being a nurse, I tended a new set of people every few hours.

Adanna went to the door. I was still standing there, holding my tea, like a numpty. Or, more precisely, like a visitor. It would take a while for me to get used to this being my house. Even longer to get used to this being my town. If I ever did.

I glanced in through the pub just as Seán strode in, a grin on his face. He stretched his hand out. Automatically, I put out mine, and he dropped the car keys into my palm. "There, and that's all sorted for you, Skye. Good as new!"

I stared at the keys to keep from staring at him. "Already? That was a lot quicker than I expected. Normally, I'd bring my car to the mechanic and get it three days later, if I'm lucky."

"Ah, well, around here we're a bit less busy, I'm thinking. As long as you don't mind used parts, things can get fixed quick, like."

Adanna cleared her throat. "Speaking of busy, I was about to give Skye a tour of her new home. Care to join us?"

A genuine expression of regret flickered across Seán's face. "Ah, much as I'd love to be in such charming company all afternoon, Sétanta will be missing me." Turning to me, he said, "You'll be welcome anytime to Ballybás, Skye. I hope you'll feel at home here in our wee village."

Sétanta? Was that his wife's name? I tried not to let disappointment color my expression.

Then he took my free hand, brought it to his lips and kissed it. I did my best not to blush, but I'm sure I failed. Maybe Sétanta wasn't his wife, then.

Once he left, I let out a long breath. Adanna chuckled. "Sure, and he's a terrible flirt. Just a warning, mind you. He's still a lovely man. Now, how about that tour of your new domain?"

Adanna gestured at the living room, or the parlour, as she called it.

"This is where your Gran was happiest, other than the bar itself. She would read each evening, a peat log burning in the fireplace."

Two walls were covered in overstuffed bookshelves, except where windows let in strong sunlight. A fireplace dominated one wall, while the other had an arched entrance to the kitchen, and several cozy chairs and sofas in between.

I furrowed my brow. "Peat? Not wood? I didn't think peat gave off light when it burned."

Giving me a wry smile, Adanna said, "That's true enough. Still, she did have electrics, you know. We have all manner of modern contrivances here in the country. Spinning jennies, electric lights, and even the telephone."

We locked gazes, and her face was completely somber. Then the corner of her mouth twitched, and I burst out in laughter. I almost spilled my tea before I placed it back on the tray. "Okay, okay, I deserved that. Now, show me the bar?"

We shuffled back into the long room. The main room was musty, but when Adanna switched the lights on, everything seemed brighter, and not just due to illumination. The place almost regained a bit of the life it must have held when it was full of people.

The bar lined one long wall, with four small round tables, mismatched chairs and stools, and tall stools at the bar itself. Behind the bar, the wall was filled with glasses, mugs, and half-empty bottles of booze. A dusty set of taps dominated the center of the bar.

"How long has this been closed?"

Adanna pursed her lips. "Since about three months before your Gran died. She just didn't have the energy to keep it up.

Sure, she could have hired staff, but staff need supervising, and she was consumed with her own self, like."

Tears suddenly pushed behind my eyes. Again, I regretted not being here for her, despite her stated wishes. "And what have folks done since then? I noticed the other pub. Is that where they go now?"

The doctor wrinkled her nose. "Aye. Most folk don't like him, but he's open. The only other pub in town closed a few years back. Your Gran's death has been a gold mine to Cormac O'Leary, without doubt. If she were a banshee, sure and she'd haunt him for that."

My skin crawled at those words. I had no idea why, but something gave me the willies. Cormac's pub? A banshee? I wasn't sure which one made me wobbly.

She turned to me with one raised eyebrow. "D'ye plan on opening the pub again? Once you're settled in, I mean."

Taking a deep breath, I said, "I have no idea. I mean, yes, that's a fantastic idea, but I've got lots to do before I can even think about it."

She patted my arm. "Fair play to you, then. The village has been itching to know ever since we found out who was getting the place."

So, I was already the subject of gossip. I supposed there wasn't much I could do about that. "What's upstairs, then?"

Adanna led me back into the parlour and up the stairs. I caressed the silky texture of the polished wood handrail. Plush maroon carpet lined each step. "Your Gran lived mostly downstairs the last month, as she couldn't climb the steps, but we had her bed moved back upstairs once she died."

"'We?'"

"That'll be me, Seán, Fionn, and Rory. They're cousins, always up for the odd job. Reliable, but… well, I wouldn't task them with anything too technical or complex."

Filing away yet another set of names, I glanced into one of the rooms upstairs. Neat as a pin, brightly lit from the sun streaming through the windows, with sage green décor. Charming and cozy. The next one was all in periwinkle. A third in soft rose. I vaguely remembered that one, and guessed we'd stayed there when I was young. "These are the B&B rooms, I'm guessing?"

"So they are. The shared bathroom is just here." She waved toward a closed door. I cracked it open and peeked inside. Not large, but also not tiny as many bathrooms were in Europe, from all I'd heard.

Adanna went back toward the stairs, then turned right and gestured toward the last door. "Now, to your Gran's suite."

My eyes grew wide. "A suite? Seriously?"

She gave a chuckle. "Well, that's what she called it. You'll see."

When she opened the dark mahogany door, I gasped. While the rest of the house had been well-kept and tastefully decorated, this room looked like a Turkish boudoir, complete with dark red damask curtains on the four-poster bed, pictures covering every inch of the maroon walls, and thick carpeting.

The room was at least three times the size of any of the guest rooms. Three windows on one wall let in plenty of light, one with a white-painted radiator beneath. The room was toasty warm, so the radiator must be on. I turned slowly, taking in all the details that my brain could process. "Wow."

"Your Gran loved her luxuries, like." My new friend wore a silly grin. "And the bathroom to fit the style?"

She opened another door and it led to a tiled bathroom with a Victorian clawed tub, decorative sink, and midnight blue and white tiles on the floor and walls. Lush blue towels hung on the rack. Even the toilet was blue and white.

"Double wow."

"Your Gran would be thrilled with that reaction. Now, let's go outside and I'll show you to the outbuildings."

I followed Adanna downstairs, but the cat pounded up the steps and almost tripped me. "Yikes!"

"Faelan, behave yourself. This is your new mistress, so be kind to her."

The cat sat at the top of the stairs, glaring down at us, his tail twitching back and forth. I wasn't sure if he disapproved of me, but the censure was clear. I'd have to take care of him for a while before he got used to me, I was sure.

Adanna gave a tour of the stone storage shed, which was empty except a few rotting bales of hay, the wooden tool shed filled with garden implements, an open shelter, and the overgrown garden. Then she let out a *tsk* and glanced at her phone. "Ah, sorry, I've got a call up in the hills. Don't forget to put a saucer of milk out here tonight. It doesn't do to ignore the wee folk. I'll have to catch up again later. Cheers!"

My head was spinning with all this new information. What had I gotten myself into?

CHAPTER FOUR

The silence that fell upon the garden as Adanna left was almost oppressive. I'd underestimated how much she talked, but her chatter had helped me keep my mind off things. New things, like my new life and my new place. Old things like Armand and my old job. A shudder ran down my spine at the memory of that final meeting with my boss, Terry. I'd felt like I was on trial, but at least I'd escaped to a new life.

But now, there was nothing keeping my mind from spiraling into a black hole of worry.

I had things to do, though. First, I unpacked my clothing, my toiletries, and the few bee things I'd kept. The bed seemed homier with my stuffed bee on the pillow.

Then, I did what I normally did when I didn't want to face my problems.

I cleaned.

Most people hate cleaning. As a nurse, I also hated it. At the same time, as a nurse, I was a fanatic about keeping things clean, despite my distaste for the chore.

The garden, however, made me wrinkle my nose. This would take more than an afternoon to set in order, and gardening was outside my wheelhouse. I'd lived in an apartment in Miami, with no lawn. Heck, we'd barely had a lawn outside the building. Everything was pavement and parking lot.

Instead, I stepped back into the parlour and did a quick assessment. Everything needed dusting. The rug smelled musty. The fireplace needed a good scrub. Okay, that's where I'd start.

But when I searched the kitchen for cleaning supplies, I came up with nothing. Nada. Zilch. Not even a roll of paper towels. Though the light did flicker a few times. I turned the switch on and off, but that didn't fix it. Maybe I needed new bulbs? These were fluorescent bulbs recessed behind frosted panels. I hadn't seen those in ages, and I wasn't confident in my ability to make that repair. Or where to buy new fluorescent bulbs. If such a thing existed.

I searched every closet I could find. Towels, sure. Bed linens a-plenty. Not one bottle of cleaning solution. Nothing for windows, wood, or rugs.

Fine. I'd need to get supplies, then. If I was going to go buy cleaning things, I'd need to get food, too.

Then I searched for a pad of paper, and found an old spiral notebook in the kitchen, and started making a list.

Bleach, window cleaner, paper towels. Toilet paper, coffee, and milk for tea. I added bread, sandwich meat, cheese, and soup. That would keep me going until I could look around and do a proper grocery run.

List in hand, I grabbed my keys and walked outside. I hesitated before locking up. Sure, this wasn't Miami, but I had no idea what sort of folks lived around here. Gran must have thought something similar, as she'd had chains installed inside each door, along with the deadbolt.

Then I stopped, having no idea where the store might be. It must be within walking distance, so I'd be foolish to drive. How far and in which direction?

I pressed my lips together, clenched my fist around the list, and marched to the main street. I half-expected to see the angry man, Brian, still glowering at the market square, but only a few people walked along the sidewalk. *Pavement, Gran said they call it the pavement here.* I would have to train myself to speak like a local.

Just on the other side of the market square, a tent sign on the sidewalk with chalk letters proclaimed milk on sale. Posters for lottery tickets were in the windows. Proud of myself for finding something without help, I strode confidently up the two steps and flung open the door.

And then bounced off Brian's chest. He glowered at me. "You, again? What do you want this time?"

He sounded so much like Armand before a fight, I had to clench my jaw to keep the anger, fear, and pain from flooding my eyes with tears.

The other man, Gerald, was behind him, so they must have been about to exit. I backpedaled out of the store and onto the pavement. I used snarky courtesy to shield my fear. "Were you just leaving? Don't let me stop you!"

Both men glared at me as they stomped away. I let out a deep breath and mounted the stairs a second time. The door jingled.

As soon as I entered, trying to make sense of the stuffed shelves in the tiny store, a cheery older woman waved. "Hello, Skye, my dear. You're welcome to Ballybás. What can I get you?"

I blinked several times, wondering if I had met this woman, but no, she was a stranger to me. Evidently my arrival was already the talk of the town. Literally.

"I just need some basic cleaning supplies. Do you have spray bleach and paper towels? And perhaps some bread and sandwich meats?"

"Oh, sure, I've got those just down this aisle."

I followed her down one corridor as she gestured to a few cleaning things. "And the food will be the next aisle over."

I couldn't help but quip, "What, all of them?"

She chuckled. "Sure, and we only have the basics here. If you want a full shopping trip, you'll have to head to Schull. That's where the SuperValu is."

I peered doubtfully at the cleaning section. There was car wax, which I hadn't seen for decades, shoe polish, which I'd never seen before in my life, and something called Fairy soap. "Schull? How far is that?"

"Just about ten, maybe fifteen minutes east of here. Most of us go there for anything fancy."

Fancy. Dish soap is fancy? With apprehension, I peeked around the corner at the grocery aisle, and determined that fancy was necessary today. I saw a few items I needed, but I'd rather get it all at once at the larger store. Still, I didn't want to just waltz in and not buy anything, so I grabbed a loaf of bread and a jar of jam.

Then I stared at the old-fashioned cash register. "Uh, do you have an ATM around? Or do you take credit?"

"Oh, sure, we can take your card." She pulled out a clunky credit card machine, and then we waited while it connected with distant satellites, and after an almost insulting length of time, decided my credit was good enough, and approved me.

I waved goodbye as I left, then realized I had never asked her name. It would be embarrassing to poke my head back in and ask, so I just resolved to ask Adanna later.

Back at the house, I put the bread and jam away, and put Schull into my phone's map app. As she said, ten minutes away. I climbed into the car and drove toward this beacon of civilization.

Or at least, I tried. As soon as I pulled out of my side street, I almost ran over a group of young men. They shouted at me and pounded the hood of my car, yelling insults. My heart jumped into my throat, and I drove carefully away, trying to stave off crying until I was well out of sight.

After a few streets, I was in the country again. As I got further away, my heart stopped pounding. They were just boys being boys, right? But my adrenaline wasn't listening.

How had I almost hit them? To be fair, I had been looking in the other direction for traffic, the way cars in America would be coming from.

When would I be able to deal with male aggression? Not that I ever had dealt with it well. My father had always yelled more than he hugged. And my mother hadn't been particularly affectionate or supportive, even when she was around. Perhaps that's why I was desperate to escape their house and jump into Armand's arms.

Something loomed in front of me, and I slammed on the brakes. When I could breathe again, I was staring at a huge tractor. It had come around a corner and we stopped inches apart. My legs were shaking as I got out of the car to make sure we didn't, in fact, hit each other. Three car crashes or almost-crashes in one day? Maybe I wasn't cut out for driving in this country.

An older farmer climbed out of the cab. "Are ye all right, pet? You were coming down that road right fast, like."

My breathing finally slowed. "I'm fine, thanks. You?"

"Ah, sure, I'm right as rain, pet. Be careful around these bends, now."

As I got back into the car, I waited a moment until my legs stopped feeling like jelly. Was every time I got into the car going to end in a near-disaster?

The tractor skirted around me, and I skirted around the tractor. We could just about make it past each other without hitting the stone wall on either side.

Then, when the coast was clear, I started my trip again… just to slam on the brakes again a minute later.

This time, a herd of sheep filled the road. With a deep sigh, I drove slowly through them, as they baaaed and skipped aside. One refused to move as I inched up closer and closer. Finally, I leaned out my window and yelled, "Shoo!"

It shooed. Slowly. Giving me a dirty look.

"Yeah, the same to you, buddy!"

As I left, I realized it was a ewe, not a ram, but I don't think she cared about being misgendered. At last, I was coming close to a town, as houses dotted the edge of the road. These houses got closer together as I drove on, and finally, I found the main street.

And then it was gone. With a mutter, I did a U turn in someone's driveway and came back, searching for the SuperValu the shopkeeper had told me of. I spied a sign and went down a side road. There! A parking lot big enough for a whole fifteen cars! Eighteen if they were all the size of my Sky-Blue Bantam.

Once inside, I had to adjust my expectation of what 'the big store' would be. This was smaller than the smallest Publix I'd ever been in. Well, at least it had an actual produce section, even if it was microscopic.

I grabbed a small cart and filled it with fruits and vegetables, vowing to eat healthier, and knowing full well that they would become science experiments in a few weeks. I also got things I *would* eat, such as cans of soup, pasta, deli meat, cheese, and more.

I stared at the frozen pizza box. Corn? On pizza? *C'mon, Skye, you said you would try new things.* So, I popped it into my cart with serious misgivings.

Irish soda bread. *That's* not something you see in Publix. I grabbed a loaf, knowing it wouldn't be as good as Gran's but still eagerly anticipating it.

Tea. Coffee. Milk. Fake sugar.

Then onto the cleaning supplies; bleach, paper towels, dishwashing liquid. Wait, did Gran have a dishwasher? I couldn't remember seeing one. Darn! Okay, well, I still needed dish soap.

Laundry soap! Almost forgot that.

After a few more impulse purchases and a candy bar, I loaded my things onto the conveyor belt, checked out, and got everything into my car. Good thing I didn't have a passenger.

On the way home, I slowed down where I had seen the flock of sheep, but the road was clear. I did, however, notice a sign on the side of the road, with a courtesy box attached. *Hamish the sheep. Photos €1.*

On the far end of that corral, an enormous ram with the biggest curved horns I'd ever seen gave me a dirty look. I laughed, waved at him, and kept driving.

Eventually, I got home, put everything away, and collapsed on the chair. I was bone-tired, and I still hadn't cleaned a darn thing.

Fortifying my strength with a cup of tea, I rested while the warm liquid helped to restore me. Once that was done, I felt ready to tackle things.

Armed with these weapons, I attacked the surfaces first, then the windows. By the time I started searching for a vacuum, I realized that dusk had fallen while I was in my cleaning frenzy. This was May, so the days were longer than I was used to in Miami. It must be past ten now.

My body ached, reminding me that yesterday had been a full travel day, and I was still subject to jet lag. Any more cleaning could wait for another day.

Should I read something? I eyed the bookshelf, noting that Gran had several puzzle books. My brain wasn't settled enough for such activity yet. Besides, I hadn't had supper yet.

Too tired to even wait for anything to cook, I slathered peanut butter and jam on bread, squished them together, and melted back into the chair. After a few moments of blissful munching, that enormous black cat jumped into my lap, almost startling a year's life out of me. "Ow! Hey! Warn a girl."

He just pawed at the sandwich and let out a yowl.

"No, Faelan. You don't get peanut butter sandwiches. I suppose you do need to be fed. Adanna said morning and night, right? I hope she left food here. I didn't think to buy some, sorry."

Climbing to my feet, I found the bag and poured some out for the cat. He glared at me. "What, you want more? You're big enough already. No more for you."

His glare became a scowl, but he finally deigned to eat some of his kibble. As he munched, I noticed a tiny splash of white on his chest.

I was about to sit back down and finish my sandwich when something yowled. It wasn't the cat this time, though. Something outside. My skin prickled and the hairs on my arm stood up.

Darkness had crept across the land while I was putting things away, and the village seemed more sinister in the gloom. Adanna had mentioned a banshee earlier, and I remembered the legend having to do with unearthly howls in the night. Or the *Sluagh Sídhe*. She said that one felt like a strong wind pushing you around. A shiver ran down my spine, in spite of knowing it was nonsense.

On a dark night in the middle of nowhere in a new country, it certainly didn't seem like nonsense.

As another howl crept down my spine, I searched frantically through the kitchen cupboards for a flashlight, and finally lifted one up. "Aha!"

It even worked.

With careful steps and a pounding heart, I crept outside, shining the flashlight down the path, and across each of the outbuildings. Shed number one, shed number two, and the shelter.

Another yowl. Half of me wanted to rush upstairs and cower under the covers. The other half was determined to be a strong woman and protect Gran's home. Besides, even a banshee would be easier to face than my ex-husband on a rage.

Something scrabbled against metal, like a raccoon in the shed. Except there were no raccoons in Ireland, were there? Maybe a squirrel. *Certainly not a banshee, silly Skye.*

But squirrels don't howl.

Another wind buffeted me and I tried hard not to think about what bizarre fairy creature might be near. As I approached the first shed, the one with garden tools, something rushed by me. My heart stopped as I jumped back and almost tumbled over the stones lining the garden edge. It ran away, but it wasn't a dog or a cat. Too big for a squirrel. What the heck had that been?

And somehow, dancing on the howling wind, came that strangely familiar music. *You must explore the shed.*

I didn't want to look in the shed. Still, if I wanted to conquer my fears, I had to face them, right? New me, new courage. My fingers were as cold as my nerves and goosebumps covered my arms as I reached out to open the door.

The metal door creaked open, the dark maw beckoning me in.

Armed with my flashlight, I shone it first in one corner, then the other, and I craned my neck in to check out the third.

And that's where the body was.

I let out a yelp and pulled back out, my heart pounding so hard, it was like thunder. I had to look again to be sure. I leaned in, gripping hard to the wall. Yes, that was definitely a body.

And one I recognized, at that. Brian, the jerk in the car earlier. He was as pale as ice.

CHAPTER FIVE

Dead silence pounded in my ears as I stared at his white face. If he had been alive, I should have been able to hear him breathe. I bent to check his pulse, but the voice of reason stopped me halfway. This could be a crime scene, and I shouldn't touch anything.

My previously ignored fear rushed back into my blood and I couldn't take it anymore. The flashlight slipped out of my hand as I pelted back to the warmth and safety of Gran's house. My house. Warm and bright and thoroughly empty of dead bodies. At least, I hoped.

Once I got my breathing back under control, I grabbed my phone. I started dialing 911, but remembered it was 999 here, and dialed that instead.

"Emergency services. What services do you require?"

Trying to pull on my nursing calm, I said, "I just found someone in my shed, and I think he's dead."

"What's your name?"

"Skye O'Shea."

"And this is at your house? What is your address?"

After I went through the comforting ritual of giving her all the information she asked for, I felt a lot better. In fact, my professional demeanor kicked in and I got curious about the body.

"We'll send over the local Gard to investigate. Do you want to stay on the line until he arrives?"

I wanted to go back and look at the body, now that my fear had dissipated. "Not unless that's required."

"Not required, but offered for people who need it."

"Then I'm fine. I am a nurse. Thank you."

After I hung up, I searched for the flashlight, but remembered I'd dropped it in the garden. I turned on the outside light so the Gard could see where he was walking, and grabbed my phone. Turning that flashlight on, I went to search for the one I dropped.

Once I retrieved it, my legs felt utterly exhausted. All the adrenaline must be draining. I stared at the shed, trying to get up the energy to examine the body. I was a nurse, right? I should be able to do so with detachment and scientific judgment.

Peeking in, I flashed the light on the dead man's face. He no longer looked angry. Almost at peace. That made me feel a bit better. Angry men were full of turmoil and chaos. His rage had fled, leaving him human again.

I couldn't see much, even by flashlight, but his skin looked incredibly pale, even for a dead person. I knew better than to touch anything.

The howl came again, sending tremors through my entire body. I aimed the light back out into the yard, but I couldn't see anything moving.

Banshees couldn't be real, could they? But this was Ireland, where stories of the fairy folk lived strong.

Just as I'd determined to go back into the house, footsteps came close.

I swung around with my light and shone it into the face of the approaching person. A tall, thin, nervous-looking man, perhaps about twenty-five, with pale, curly hair squinted at me. "Skye O'Shea? You called for the Gard? I'm Gard McCarthy"

Swallowing, I nodded. "I did. I found a body in my shed."

Gard McCarthy flipped open a notebook and clicked his pen, looking at me expectantly. "Right. How long ago did you discover the body?"

I swallowed and glanced toward the shed. "Just a few minutes before I called it in."

"And did you touch the body?"

His manner was getting on my already-jangling nerves already. "I most certainly did not."

He glanced up, his eyebrows raised. "Are you sure the person is dead?"

Crossing my arms, I said, "No, I'm not sure. But I was a nurse, so I have seen plenty of dead bodies."

"You *were* a nurse, were you? And why aren't you a nurse now?"

I had no wish to discuss that particular incident in my past with a stranger, Gard or not. "I don't see how that's relevant."

Gard McCarthy grumbled something that sounded like, *typical O'Shea nonsense.* Then he turned his back on me and knelt by the body.

As he examined the body and took notes, I debated returning to the house. Despite the summer season, I was chilled to the bone. As much as I wanted the safety and warmth, I couldn't leave. I needed to bear witness to this man and his death. Perhaps it was a nurse thing, the need to be there for someone, even if they were an obnoxious twit.

Looking up from his pad, McCarthy said, "You should go inside, Mrs. O'Shea."

I shook my head. "No, I'm fine."

He frowned at me. "I'm not as concerned about your mental state as about the crime scene, and any footprints you're trampling across."

I stared at my feet, firm upon the flagstones. Then my stubborn streak kicked in and I straightened my shoulders. "I'm a nurse. I know better than to contaminate the scene, Gard McCarthy."

"That's as may be, Mrs. O'Shea…"

"*Miss* O'Shea, please. I'm not married." Well, *almost* not married, but that wasn't the issue here. Besides, I was practicing the correction to my title.

He pursed his lips. "*Miss* O'Shea, then. You certainly do seem as mulish as your grandmother. Go back into the house. I don't want you distracting me as I process the scene. Is that a good enough reason for you? Or do I need to take you into the station?"

"I didn't realize it was a violation to stand in my garden, crime scene or not."

His voice took on a nasty edge that sounded just like Armand in a yelling mood. "You've a neck, no question. It is a violation if you're obstructing an investigation. Go inside and wait for me there. I will need to question you after this."

That tone made me want to cower, obey, and make myself as small as possible. Still, I was determined to stand strong, so I glared at him with my arms crossed. Time to channel my Gran. "Oh, forgive me, Gard McCarthy, for daring to stand in my yard. I wouldn't want to mess up your little detective game. Wouldn't want to hinder your brilliant investigative skills with my *obstructing presence.*"

I was shivering in the cold and would be much more comfortable inside. His bullying attitude, tapping into memories

I didn't want to face, had my hackles up, and I didn't feel like giving in to such tactics.

The chill in his voice should have made snow fall. "Miss O'Shea, if you are so insistent, we can start the questioning." With a surprisingly gentle hand, he led me to the porchlight and pulled his pad back out, pencil ready. "How did you find the body?"

"I heard a noise. Some sort of howling animal. I came outside to investigate."

He wrote in his notebook. "And why did you look in the shed?"

"Something ran from the shed past me. Maybe a cat or a squirrel or something. I went in to see if they'd done any damage."

"Uh-huh. And was anyone else with you?"

"No, I was alone."

He peered at me over his glasses. "You came out on a dark night, in a new town, alone? Investigating mysterious sounds?"

Rolling my eyes, I replied, "Yes, I came out alone. I grew up in the city. I've faced down muggers and gunmen. I wasn't too concerned over a squirrel bent on destruction."

"Hm. Right, then what happened?"

"I shone my flashlight into the shed, into each corner. He was in the third corner."

"And do you recognize the victim?"

"Yes, his name is Brian. I met him briefly this morning."

He glanced up at that, his eyebrows raised. "How did you meet? Is he a friend?"

My temper was beginning to fray, and I wanted this to be over. My tone turned snappish. "We met because his car hit my car. He is definitely not a friend. Wait, I did see him once before that, at a castle on the way here from Dublin. But we barely exchanged a few words."

"What's his last name?"

"I have no idea what his last name is. Didn't Seán tell you about this? Your wife told him to."

He pressed his lips into a thin line. "It is not Seán's duty to report an accident involving two vehicles that he was not involved in. It is your responsibility to do so."

He was right, and I knew it. Even though I didn't want to admit it. I stared at my hands, clasped tight in front of me. "I was a bit out of sorts. Adanna brought me here and plied me with tea until I felt better."

Gard McCarthy let out a sigh and rolled his eyes. "I'll discuss that with her later. Did you exchange insurance information?"

"I…" Then I realized that I hadn't done so. "No, I guess I didn't. I must have been more rattled than I realized. He had two people with him, but they left after he started getting angry. Then Adanna and Seán showed up."

That surprised him again. "Oh?"

"Yes. She took me home while Seán went to get my taillight fixed."

"Then what did you do?"

Taking a deep breath, I calmed my temper. "I was going to start cleaning the house but lacked cleaning supplies and any food. So, I went to the shop. She didn't have what I needed so I went to the nearby town. Schull, I think?"

"And when did you return from Schull? Can anyone vouch for your whereabouts?"

That cold feeling started creeping through my blood, like when I was being questioned at the hospital. "Sometime in the afternoon. Vouch? Am I a suspect?"

Gard McCarthy tapped his notebook. "You should be. Especially after leaving the scene of the accident, and the other party to that accident showing up dead in your shed."

My nerves were beginning to crawl. "I didn't have anything to do with this! I don't even know him!"

With a scowl, he said, "But you did. As you just described. You had an altercation with a man who was later found dead on your property. That's suspicious even with every benefit of the doubt one might fabricate."

I ground my teeth, unable to think of a good answer to that. "Do you think that I would go and kill a stranger, then drag him onto my property, and then call him in? Do you think I'm a complete idiot?"

He snapped his notebook shut. "My opinion of you is not at issue. The facts are all I care about. However, at this time, I don't have enough to charge you. Still, I need to be informed of your movements, especially as you had an altercation with the victim."

Then someone else approached, with another light. As they came closer, I recognized her. Adanna, still looking as if she were wearing all green, though it was too dark to see any colors. Maybe her previous outfit had imprinted on my memory so strongly, she'd always be *green* to me. That had happened in the past, strongly associating a particular color to a person. My hackles began to smooth down.

She glanced between me and Gard McCarthy. "Skye? Are you alright? Dónal, what happened?"

Dónal? Oh, right. I'd forgotten that they were married. Adanna would be here as the doctor, to declare the body dead. "I'm fine. I just didn't want to go back into the house yet."

That was definitely a lie, and I was staying out of spite now, but she gave me an excuse. "After I take a sconce at the victim, please let me take you inside. You look half-frozen."

I felt weak for admitting that. After all, this was summer, wasn't it? Well, May, at least. In Miami, I'd be sweating profusely, even at night. Here, the wind blew chilly once the sun went down. I gave a meek nod.

Adanna walked into the shed. I was tempted to watch her examination, but suddenly, I wanted nothing to do with the body. Then she came out, wrote up her findings under the porch light, and handed it to the Gard.

"Right, in we go. We'll have some tea."

It was a command not to be disobeyed.

CHAPTER SIX

Adanna sat me down in the comfy chair and went into the kitchen to make tea. Water in the kettle; cups from the cupboard. She must have found the milk and sugar, for when she came in with a full tray, she was beaming. "Looks like you're all stocked now, that's grand. You've had a fright tonight. Want to talk about it?"

I shook my head. "Not just yet. Your husband already drained me with his questions."

She wrinkled up her nose. "Aye, well, he's a stickler for the rules, and sometimes his diplomacy leaves a bit to be desired. Sometimes he acts like an eejit, sure enough. Fine, then. Shall I distract you with gossip or with tales?"

That piqued my interest. "What sort of tales?"

She leaned back in the settee. "I could relate some about local legends, if you like."

Her voice was soothing to my prickly nerves. "That sounds fantastic."

"Well, the first I can relate is about the *Fear Dearg.*"

"You mentioned that one before, when you spoke of the old sheep farmer."

She gave a sly grin. "Padraig, yes. He complains about them constantly. The Fear Dearg, you see, is a trickster. A nasty sort he is, too. He will play practical jokes, but not harmless ones. They can be a right terror, if not appeased."

The Fear Dearg hardly sounded pleasant. "What do these Fear Dearg look like?"

"Well, the name translates from the Irish as 'Red Man,' as he wears a red cap and coat. He's a dirty, hairy creature, fat with a long nose. Maybe even a tail like a rat."

I hated rats. There had been rats at my first apartment. That shiver returned and goosebumps rose on my arms. I tried to rub them away. "And how does one appease them?"

"Well, if you suspect a Fear Dearg is trying to trap you, then the best way to prevent that is to say 'do not mock me'. It's better in the Irish, of course."

"What's the Irish?"

"Na dean magadh fum."

"Nah den maga foom?" The sounds felt strange on my tongue.

She visibly tried not to giggle. "Close enough."

Fairies weren't real. Everyone knew that. Nonetheless, I repeated the phrase in my mind, committing it to memory. Just in case.

The teapot whistled, and Adanna went to fetch it. When she returned, we waited for the tea to brew.

"Then there's the *Dearg-Due*, to keep with the theme of red."

"What's that one, then? And what's the fascination with red?"

Adanna gave a smile. "Red's the color of blood, so it is. A sacred color, of course. Long, long ago, there was a lovely girl with blood-red lips and blond hair. Men traveled from far and wide to see her beauty and win her hand. However, she fell in love with a local farmer, and her father was greedy. He sold her hand to a cruel man three times her age."

I let out a snort of disgust.

"The girl's new husband delighted in torturing her, including drawing her blood and locking her in the tower."

I peeked at the tea, but it needed more brewing. "Rather typical of most fairy tales, I'd guess."

"Right you are. So, she waited for her farmer love to rescue her, but he never did. In despair, she starved herself by hiding her scran each day."

"Wait, what was that word? Scran?"

"Scran? Oh, that's food. When she died, she denounced God and vowed vengeance. The townspeople failed to pile a cairn over her grave, which allowed her spirit to walk free."

That darned shiver came back. "What sort of vengeance? And upon whom?"

Adanna tapped her temple. "That would be upon any man. She became the Dearg-Due, the drinker of red blood. Much like vampire stories."

Then I remembered how pale Brian's face had been in my shed, and rubbed the goosebumps away once again. "An Irish vampire. Huh, I had no idea."

"Another type would be the *cat sídhe,* of course."

Faelan the cat chose that moment to leap on my lap and settled down with a purr louder than the tractor I'd almost hit that afternoon. Adanna and I exchanged a glance and a grin at his perfect timing. It helped lighten my mood a lot.

"Tell me about the cat sídhe."

"They are much larger than the mundane sort. Long tails, usually black or dark green with a white spot on their chest. A few are white with red ears, but those are usually Brigid's creatures."

"Brigid?"

"She's a goddess or a saint, depending on who you ask. She's associated with creativity, blacksmithing, all sorts of things."

We both looked at Faelan again. As I pet his thick fur and my hand traveled down his back and his very long tail, I asked, "And what do they do?"

"Some say it can steal the souls of the dead, which is why we perform a wake, making sure the cat doesn't walk over their corpse." We glanced toward the door and Adanna cleared her throat. "But more often that they can see through illusions or transform nine times. Sometimes, it's more that the creature is a human witch transformed into a cat."

"Nine times? Is that where the idea of nine lives comes from?"

"Possibly."

Faelan twitched his tail and let out a growl, then leapt off my lap, disappearing into the shadows again.

Just as he did so, something howled in the distance. My skin prickled again. "Tell me you heard that, too, Adanna."

The doctor gave a solemn nod. "That would be the Bean Sídhe, more likely than not. There has been death this night, so she'll be awake and moaning about, like."

So many words scrambled in my mind, I couldn't speak. Weren't banshees attached to a family? And how could anyone distinguish the wail of a banshee from the constant wind? Instead, I sipped my tea, almost grown tepid by now. "You're a doctor, though. Surely you can't believe in all this stuff?"

She sipped her tea. "Of course not. Still, in matters of the Otherworld, it's wise to keep an open mind."

As I mulled that apparent contradiction, I took another sip of tea. It was too cold now, so I warmed it with a splash of water from the teapot.

"Now, Skye, tell me about yourself. Everyone is itching to hear your story."

Today must be the day of spinal shockwaves, because this didn't sit well with me at all. I'd spent all my life in Miami, where everyone was a stranger. No one cared about your life. That sort of anonymity was a shield, protection against pain.

But Gran had told me many times that small town life was different. Everyone knew everything about everyone. Now, it was my turn to share.

I let out a deep breath. "My story. Well, you know that I lived in Miami, right? Born and raised there. Mom brought me here to Gran's at least annually when I was a child. When she passed away, though, that stopped."

"Was she in an accident?"

I shook my head. "No, it was cancer. In fact, that may have been why I decided to be a nurse. I wanted to fix her so badly."

Adanna placed a hand on my forearm. "I'm so sorry, Skye. What about your father?"

Letting out a snort, I shook my head. "He's dead, too, and good riddance."

The doctor sucked in her breath, her eyes growing wide.

I waved my hand. "No, really. He was an abusive brute, and I'm well rid of him. So, what about you? Are you born and bred here?"

"No, my family's from here, but I grew up in Dublin. I worked as a diagnostician but got tired of the back-stabbing ambitious types, so fled to the farm, as it were."

We spent another half hour chatting about pleasant things and finally, Adanna excused herself. "You seem much more settled now. I'm beginning to fade, so I'll let you go."

Headlights played across the windows and for a moment, the panic returned, but I made myself breathe evenly, and it faded.

"If I'm not mistaken, that'll be the coroner from Schull come to take the victim."

When Adanna left, I put away the tea things. Voices outside caught my attention. Despite my revulsion, I was curious, so I sidled up to the back door as close as I could to listen. Their voices were muffled, but I heard most of it.

A new voice said, "I've never seen anything quite like this, Dónal. All the blood, not just a pint or two."

Gard McCarthy answered, "Could it be some sort of ritual thing?"

"I haven't a clue. I'll search the back records. If I find anything during the autopsy, you'll be the first to know."

All the blood was drained? That was very odd. I couldn't think of any disease that would cause that, and it would be darned difficult to do, even with modern equipment. And why?

Unless the tales about Dearg-Due were true.

Ridiculous. Now I was just jumping at shadows. Literally, because Faelan chose that moment to pounce on my toes.

"Cat! Stop that now!"

He meowed and marched up the stairs. I took his hint and trudged up the stairs. I'd unpacked my clothes earlier, but now I couldn't find where I'd put my pajamas, so just found a t-shirt and some shorts and slipped under the covers.

Instead of falling asleep, as my exhausted body craved, I stared at the ceiling as an almost-full moon shone through the upstairs window. It felt so odd sleeping in Gran's bed. Not that I was superstitious about her ghost or anything, but I did feel like an intruder upon her haven, her domain. I wondered if I'd ever get used to this place.

Reasons for exsanguination ran through my mind. Blood was drawn during a phlebotomy, of course, but only enough to test. If the artery was cut, the victim would bleed out in a few minutes, but there would still be blood in the body, just not enough to maintain life. Embalmers removed blood during their preparations, but they replaced it with embalming fluid.

Then memories of the hospital flickered by. The comforting, acrid smell of antiseptic. The syringe with the medicine I was supposed to administer. The nagging doubt which still haunted me…

Heavy weight jumped on my chest. Silver moonlight showed the outline of the cat. With a grunt, I said, "Darn it, Faelan! Will you warn a person next time?"

He licked his paw with precise grace and spoke in a growling voice. "I will not."

Somehow, I levitated out from under the covers and my back was against the door before I could even yell in surprise. "Holy sheep nuggets! Did you just talk?!"

Faelan cocked his head at me. "Of course, I did. Has your ancestor never spoken of me?"

"How the heck can you talk?"

The cat narrowed his eyes. "Because I can. How can you talk?"

I shook my head, trying to make sense of his words. "This doesn't make sense. Cats don't talk."

"Are you still on that? She never told me you were stupid." He resumed licking his paw.

I grabbed my head and dug my fingers into my hair. "No, no, I must be asleep. This is a dream, right?"

The cat just stared at me.

I started pacing, shaking my head. Then I slapped my cheek, but nothing changed. I pinched the skin on the back of my left hand, but the pain didn't wake me, either.

Faelan let out a faint hiss, then returned to licking his paw. "You are of her lineage, so of course you have the same powers as she did."

I halted mid-stride and stared at him. "Powers? What powers? But… wait, are you one of those cat sídhe Adanna was talking about?"

He stopped licking and looked up. After a few heartbeats, he said, "I would have thought that much obvious, even to you. As to your powers, I cannot tell you. You must discover those on your own. If you aren't too stupid."

This couldn't be happening. I'd fallen asleep, and this was all a dream, right? I pinched the skin on my forearm. It stung, but I was still staring at the cat.

His tail whipped back and forth, and there was a faint growl below his voice. "I don't have a great deal of time. I can only speak occasionally, so listen, even if you don't believe me yet."

"Fine. I'll listen, but when I wake up..."

"Silence, human! This is important. The dead human caused his demise."

"You mean, he committed suicide?"

"No. He caused his death. You must look into the past to find the future." The cat's head whipped toward the window. "Meow. Grrowl."

A cloud now shrouded the moon, and the cat sounded like any enormous tom angry at something.

Well, that was as clear as mud. "That's it? Nothing else?"

Faelan's back rose and he hissed, then settled in the middle of the bed, curled up and went to sleep.

I couldn't sleep myself. Instead, I prowled around the house, unsettled and nervous. I checked all the doors to make certain they were secure. I listened in the night for that howling, but heard nothing. No movement in the back garden, especially near the sheds. Finally, I dragged myself up the stairs again and stared at the cat in the center of the bed.

I wanted to shove him off out of sheer frustration, then I remembered the golden rule when it came to fairies. Don't make them angry. You wouldn't like them when they're angry.

Fine. I grabbed an extra blanket from the wardrobe and lie on the far edge, not disturbing the sleeping, frustrating cat.

How would a fairy cat, if that's what he was, know anything about the dead man in the shed? Or how he'd been killed. Faelan said it wasn't suicide, but that Brian had caused his death, so perhaps he'd made someone else so angry, they murdered him? I could understand that in a visceral way, having encountered his rage.

Gran's cat was a fairy. Did that mean Gran was a fairy, too? Or at least, she could speak with fairies. Did that make Gran evil? A witch? Something else?

And if that was true, what did it make me?

I must have tripped through a looking-glass when I wasn't looking. Maybe Adanna had laced my tea with LSD.

Somewhere in the midst of my churning thoughts, I finally slept, with dreams Lewis Carroll would have been proud of.

Faelan appeared out of formless darkness, grinning like the Cheshire Cat.

CHAPTER SEVEN

The next morning, I had no idea where I was. I glanced around at the Celtic knotwork decorations, the Brigid's cross on the wall, and the photographs, and it all clicked into place. Gran's bedroom.

I stretched and winced as my muscles ached. I was in the car too long yesterday, after being on the plane too long the day before, and my body was in full revolt. I promised it a nice, hot shower, but it didn't stop whining.

Well, that was the plan, anyhow. I stared at the bathroom knobs and the switch and the timer and wondered what the heck all this was about. I fiddled with the knobs, but nothing happened. Then I tried the switch, and something started humming, but no water came. Then I turned the timer. It noisily clicked, and the light above turned on. A trickle of water appeared. Trying the knobs for a second time, I finally got some water from the shower head.

But it was ice-cold.

I let it run for a bit, hoping it would get warmer, and tackled my hair with the brush. By the time the tangles were tamed, I tested the water again. It had gotten reasonably hot, so I climbed in. Then the timer stopped ticking and everything went dark.

Also, the water was getting cold again.

Growling, I turned the timer back on, all the way around, which was a half hour. Then the water grew warmer, the lights came on, and I finished my hot shower while I still could.

Once fresh and clean, I dressed in a bee t-shirt and some jeans and padded downstairs for some breakfast. While I would love something hot, I was in no mood to cook. I rarely was, truth be told. Lazy in the kitchen, that's what Armand always called me.

After grabbing the box of cereal and milk I bought the day before, I poured both in a bowl and then fished a spoon out of the drawer. I held the bowl while I ate, wandering around the parlour. I glanced again at the puzzle books. My mind might be ready for those after breakfast.

Something caught my eye in the back garden, and I glanced out the window. Had the Gard come back to examine the scene in the daylight? But I didn't see anyone there. Maybe Faelan or some other animal.

Had Faelan talked to me last night? Or was it some strange jet-lagged dream? It had to be the latter, didn't it?

Something moved again in the garden. After putting my bowl down, I went outside to see what it was. I peered into the herb section, the flower beds, and the potato garden, but nothing stirred. Not even the wind, and that was unusual indeed for western Ireland, at least from what Gran had said.

Taking a deep breath, I poked my head into the shed. There was a lot of dirt and debris inside, and it was obvious Gran hadn't used it in quite a while. The dirt had a big depression in the corner where Brian had been lying.

"*Miss* O'Shea. You're trespassing on a crime scene."

I spun to find Gard McCarthy glaring at me, his arms crossed and his toe tapping. I wanted to laugh at the stereotypical annoyed cop posture, but instead, I asked, "Did you find anything with the body last night? I was thinking of ways someone could have… killed him."

I almost said, *ways someone could have drained all his blood*, then I remembered I'd learned that bit of intelligence from eavesdropping, and the Gard didn't know I had that data. He already thought poorly of me, and that would make things worse.

To his credit, he kept his tone respectful. "That's my job, Miss O'Shea. Please stop trampling on the evidence. Thank you."

I backed up several steps, but still stared at the ground near the shed door. Now the Gard's tone turned testy. "Don't you have something else you should be doing?"

"Other than examining my backyard?"

"Other than interfering with an investigation, yes. If you insist on pushing yourself into my space, I'll have to take you into the station. Just to keep you out of my hair, mind you."

I held up my hands in surrender. "Fine. I'll leave you to it, then." With a straight spine, I marched back to the house, seething but knowing better than to make it worse. This time.

Once inside again, I tried to figure out what to do next to keep my mind off the murder. The cleaning supplies glared at me, and I glared right back. I didn't have the energy to clean just now.

I rarely had much leisure time. Between my nursing job and caring for Armand, I never found a way to keep myself busy or take up a hobby. Now, with Gran's place to live in, I had no rent to pay. Her estate would keep me going for a while before I needed to start bringing in money myself, with the pub and the B&B. Perhaps in a year or so, if I was careful with my spending.

I definitely wanted to get it going again. After all, I owed it to Gran to keep her legacy strong. That would take a lot of work. I would never get it all done overnight.

Which meant I could take some time to just relax, a foreign concept to me. Still, I deserved some self-care, with all that I'd been going through.

With that in mind, I treated myself to a stroll through the village, taking in the sights.

The town was mostly around one main street through the center, though Gran's pub was about a half block down a side street. The other pub, O'Leary's, was about three times the size of Gran's, with fresh paint, slick decorations, and a well-lit sign. Also, lots of parking out back.

Maybe I shouldn't open Gran's pub, after all. I couldn't compete with O'Leary's glitzy place, right on the main street. O'Shea's was tucked away in a side street and would need lots of cash to upgrade to that level. Gran had left me some funds, but not enough for all that.

But I had a duty to Gran. I needed to at least give it a try.

Along the main street, there was the corner shop I visited yesterday, the green post office, a launderette, the Gard station. The clinic, which must be where Adanna worked. I also noticed a gallery, a few gift shops, a café, and a few other shops along the side roads. I glimpsed a sign for a pizza place, a chemist, and a salon. There were a few shuttered buildings here and there.

At the end of the street was a petrol station and garage, which is presumably where Seán had taken my car to be repaired yesterday.

I wanted to talk with Adanna, but I didn't want to monopolize her time. Instead, I went into the corner grocery. The same older woman as yesterday was at the register, and she probably ran the place.

"Oh, did you find the SuperValu, yesterday, dear?"

"I did, thank you."

"I'm so glad. What can I get you here today, then?"

I glanced around, not sure what I was craving, but my eyes fell upon some candy bars. "I think I need some chocolate, but I'm not as familiar with Irish brands."

She tapped her chin and stared at the candy rack. "There's Cadbury Dairy Milk, of course, but you'll have that in the States, won't ye? And Crunchie, that's got honeycomb. Mars, Twix, Snickers, those are all common enough. Boost, do you have those? It has caramel and biscuit inside, it's class. Flake is a thin sheet of chocolate all crinkled up."

"The Boost sounds delightful. I'll take one of those."

The door opened and the priest walked in. "G'morning, lass." Then he turned to the other woman. "Has the paper come in yet?"

The shop owner nodded toward the paper stand. "Just put them out, Father."

As I paid for my candy bar, the priest came to stand next to me, a paper in his hand. "You're Skye O'Shea, is that right? Just moved into Saoirse's Pub?"

"Yes, that's right. Saoirse was my Gran."

A grin split his face. "You're very welcome here, then. I'll come by later this afternoon for a proper greeting and stories over tea. Will that suit you?"

I swallowed but it would be churlish to refuse, and I wanted to make a good impression, despite Gard McCarthy. "Of course, Father. What time?"

"Brilliant! Say, 2:30 for 3?"

I wrinkled my brow. "I beg your pardon?"

"Oh, sorry. That means I'll be there between 2:30 and 3. An Irish phrase, as it happens."

"That's great. I'll see you then."

I made a mental note to make sure the parlour was clean. I'd done some work yesterday, but never finished. I didn't like unfinished jobs, but yesterday was chock full.

As I left the shop, I strolled back down the street, examining the storefronts more closely. I waved to a woman with long, fly-away red-blond hair and round-rimmed glasses, and she waved back. The sunlight seemed to paint her yellow, like the summer sun.

Then to a younger woman with burgundy hair done up in a ponytail on top of her head, like a fountain, but she was staring intently at her phone as she walked, and almost stumbled into a signpost.

An old pick-up truck with two young men drove slowly by. One of them said something to the woman with the ponytail. She gave them a rude gesture, but with a smile, so I figured it was friendly banter.

I found myself in front of Adanna's clinic again, but just as I'd turned to head back down the street, she poked her head out. "Skye! Come here to me! I was just about to take a break."

I wouldn't mind a chance to talk about the murder with Adanna. At least she wouldn't treat me like a second-rate criminal, like Gard McCarthy. She was a doctor, so she'd be able to discuss the medical ideas I had. "I don't want to bother you, if…"

"Don't be silly. I need a break. It's been a day already, let me tell you."

As I entered, I glanced around the small clinic. A waiting room painted in soothing pale blue, some second-hand stuffed waiting chairs and an empty desk. Then, inside the actual office, an examination table, computer, sink, and lots of broken glass.

I stared at the glass. "Adanna, what happened? Are you okay?" Window glass, from the look of it. But there were some curved bits, as well. Bottles?

She waved it off. "I'm fantastic, no worries. Dónal will be here when he's done up in the hills at Padraig's place. He said someone stole one of his sheep last night and is in a right froth about it."

The window had been shattered in, and the locker with medicines pried open. There were unbroken bottles jumbled together on the floor amidst the glass. "Can I help clear things up, at least?"

Doctor Adanna shook her head with a sour frown. "I've done what I can. Dónal said to leave the rest until he can look at it." She sat on the stool, her hands in her lap, and gave a grin. "I know *how* to wait. I know I shouldn't touch anything. That doesn't mean I like it!"

I didn't see any blood on the broken glass, so whoever had shattered the window used a tool other than their hands. "Was it like this when you arrived? Did you see anyone? Did they get anything valuable?"

"Not a soul. No, I keep the expensive drugs in the locker here, and that's still intact."

Remembering the day before, I asked, "I noticed a group of rough-looking young men yesterday. They were jeering at me and hit my car as I went by. Do you know them?"

She waved that suggestion away. "Ah, they're just lads. No harm in them. This was probably just some young swain looking to impress his mates with a bit of danger. These things happen sometimes, even in the country."

"And what about the two other people who were with Brian? Maybe they were involved?"

She wrinkled her brow. "Brian?"

I stared at her. "The dead man in my garden? Did you forget?"

Adanna let out a chuckle. "Ah, him. Sorry, forgot his name. What other two people?"

"The ones in the car with him." Then I remembered that they had escaped before anyone else had arrived, so Adanna probably never even saw them.

The doctor seemed much too cavalier about this break-in, even if she was married to the Gard. "What did they take? Have you had a chance to take an inventory?"

Her expression turned pensive, and she stared at the medicine locker. "It doesn't look like much, really. Some bottles of pain meds. An astringent. Some hypodermic needles. Some other small bits. Nothing expensive, and more supplies and equipment than drugs. I won't know for certain until I can put everything in order."

Carefully, I looked out the window, avoiding the sharp edges still in the pane. I saw some scuffling in the dirt outside, and without even saying anything, went out the front door to examine it.

Someone had been there, and there was darker dirt, almost reddish in color. Definitely different than the sandy-colored dirt in the flower bed in front of the clinic. "Adanna? Do you—"

At that moment, Dónal pulled up, a mighty frown upon his face. "What are you doing here?"

Pulling my shoulders back, I said, "Helping my friend. What about you? Why weren't you here helping her, as well?"

He gave out a snort. "I have a duty to everyone in this village, not just my wife."

I scowled at him as he went inside. I thought it the better part of wisdom to make tracks out of there before Gard McCarthy got snippy again.

A woman's raised voice behind me caught my attention. I turned to see the shopkeeper admonishing a man about her age. From his hangdog expression and slumped shoulders, I guessed that must be her husband, and he'd done something very wrong.

Even a small argument between strangers made me anxious. I kept my head down as I passed them. A soft mist of rain fell as their voices faded behind me.

CHAPTER EIGHT

As I walked back down the main street, things jumbled in my mind. The burglars had pried open one locker, but a second one was untouched. That one, Adanna said, held the more expensive drugs. Maybe they just didn't have a chance to get to it, or didn't realize it held a greater prize? Perhaps they were worried about getting caught and ran away.

Most of the things gone were equipment, rather than drugs. I still thought it might be the kids who'd given me a hard time. Then again, there might be more than one rough group in town, even in this small of a place. A thousand people could mean plenty of folks younger than twenty.

Footsteps were hurrying up behind me, and I turned to see Adanna running up, something in her hand. "Skye! You forgot this."

I stared at my car keys. I didn't even realize I had them with me. "Thanks!" I took them from her and she hesitated, so I didn't turn away.

"What? Did you remember something else?"

"Well, you asked about two people with Brian, right? The victim?"

I gave a cautious nod.

Adanna pressed her lips together. "I *did* see him the day before you arrived. He was in O'Leary's with a young woman."

I raised my eyebrows. "Do you remember what she looked like?"

Staring down the street at nothing, the doctor said, "Tall and thin. Black hair, straight, well past her shoulders, wearing a bright yellow dress. I wish I could get away with that color. But it would just wash my complexion to nothing."

"Focus, Adanna. What else?"

She gave a shrug. "I didn't recognize her, then again, I hadn't recognized him, either. I figured they were just another couple on holiday. We get so many people here for just a few hours. Maybe a day or three, if they're bored. Most stay further east, in Cork City or Kenmare."

"And they were together, like a couple?"

She shrugged. "They sat at the same table. I can't remember if they were acting in love or not. I don't think they were even talking to each other much. They both had drinks, that's about all I can recall. I'd been drinking a bit myself at that point."

"Fair enough. If you do remember anything else about her, can you let me know? I'd like to talk to her, if I can find her. I think he called her Cherie."

Adanna gave a nod and glanced toward her clinic. "I'll do that. I'd better return, though. Lunch break is long over."

She hurried back down the street, and I stared at her for a few moments before turning toward home. Well, to Gran's home. I still couldn't get used to calling it my home. It might be a while before that happened.

Once inside, I looked around for Faelan, but didn't see him anywhere. Probably skulking in some shadows, or whatever fairy cats did during daylight hours.

Now, however, I had the energy and the impetus to do more cleaning, especially with the priest coming over that afternoon. So, I found my new-bought supplies and decided to start with the parlour.

Then I remembered I still had my keys in my hand. Exasperated, I searched around for a good spot for them to live. If I put my keys and purse in the same place every day, I was much less likely to lose them. I had been dropping my purse on the kitchen counter, but that was less than hygienic. Purse bottoms were cesspools of bacteria.

Out of the corner of my eye, I spied some hooks on the wall in the hallway. Upon closer examination, I found five hooks, and one held a large ring of keys, antique and rusty. Most were skeleton keys with long barrels and ornate bows at the base. A few were medium-sized, plain, and a bit more modern. One was tiny, with a flower carved out of the bow. Something within me urged me to pick them up.

A faint strain of music played somewhere. Did someone have windchimes on their porch? Maybe someone was driving by with their radio on? But when I went out the front pub door, I didn't see anyone on the street. Maybe it was just the metal keys jingling.

I tried each key in the pub door, but none of them fit. Then I tried them in the back door and each of the garden sheds. Still, no joy.

I wanted to check each of the interior doors, but realized that if I didn't start cleaning soon, the priest would arrive, and I wouldn't be anywhere near finished. Besides, they probably only fitted Faelan's magic fairy box or something equally unlikely.

Reluctantly, I hung them back up on the hooks. My keys looked depressingly modern next to the charming older keys.

Even more reluctantly, I grabbed the dust rag and furniture polish, and tackled all Gran's wooden furniture in the parlour. Once I was done with that, I cleaned the windows, inside and out, and then vacuumed the carpet. Just as I turned it off, there was a knock at the door.

With a frantic glance at the wall clock, I hurried to the door. I must have lost track of time! And I hadn't even brushed my hair, so I must look a mess.

Then I took a deep breath and reminded myself that a priest is not a gaggle of judgmental older ladies looking for malicious gossip. Even in a small town. At least, I hoped not.

I opened the door and put on my most charming smile. "Father Fraser! Thank you so much for coming. Please, excuse my appearance. I've been cleaning everything that stays put long enough." As if to punctuate my words, the lights flickered.

He let out a chuckle, and I realized he spoke with a lovely Scottish accent. "You're fine, lass. I suppose I'd better keep moving while I'm here, then?"

I led him into the parlour and said, "I'll just put the kettle on." That's what they always said in the Irish movies and shows, right? It seemed right to me.

As I went through the motions of filling the kettle, putting it on the ancient stove burner, and filling the tray with cups, saucers, milk, sugar, and spoons, I realized the little ritual helped to calm me. I wondered if that was part of the reason for the tradition.

Throughout history, it was a mark of hospitality to offer a drink to a visitor. Especially for Irish and Scottish folks. Also, it was a mark of trust, showing you weren't poisoning anyone.

Besides, it was the neighborly thing to do. I didn't want my Gran haunting me for not being neighborly.

I brought the tray out, just like Adanna had done the day before, and settled in the comfy chair I'd adopted as my favorite. Father Fraser was perched on the settee, glancing around. "It doesn't look like you've changed much since you arrived."

"Oh, did you visit often?"

He gave a wry smile. "Not as much as I wanted to. Your Gran didn't come to Mass, you see, despite plenty of urging."

I gave a low chuckle. "Once she made up her mind about something, neither hell nor high water would shift her from her decision."

"That is indeed God's own truth. Now, tell me about yourself, Miss O'Shea. You just moved here from America, is that correct?"

"Please, call me Skye." At that moment, the kettle started screeching, so I hurried to the kitchen to fetch it, scowled at the flickering lights, and came back to pour the tea. While I did that, I formed my response in my mind. I didn't want to blabber on about myself like I usually did.

I hadn't done so with Adanna, but that's because she was a talker herself, and I rarely got a word in edgewise. But a priest was trained to listen. That was one of his main jobs. Even if I hadn't been a practicing Catholic for many years.

That was something else I shouldn't tell him. My hands felt sweaty, and I surreptitiously wiped them on my slacks. "Yes, I moved here from Miami, as soon as I could get all the visas and paperwork sorted. That was a bit of a tangled mess, too."

He added milk to his tea, but no sugar. I added some of both. I couldn't handle the tannins in tea without sugar to soften them.

The Father pressed his lips into a thin line. "Ireland certainly doesn't make it easy for people to emigrate. Even from the UK."

"You're from Scotland, Adanna says, yes?"

"I am, from up in the highlands. Well, in Perth, at any rate. On the south edge of the highlands."

I took a sip of tea, anything to keep my hands busy. Why was I so nervous around him?

"And do you have any family? Will they be joining you?"

Ah, the oh-so-innocent question. His expression was utterly guileless, but this was the part I was dreading. *Stick to the facts, Skye. Don't elaborate.* "No, I have no family."

Irish Catholics didn't look kindly upon divorce. Even if the husband was an abusive slime. Time to change the subject, stat.

"Oh, I wanted to ask you! What is the shopkeeper's name? She knew mine, and I didn't want to ask her. It seemed rude."

A smile split his face. "Ah, that would be Máiréad Flaherty. She runs the shop and the post office with her husband. She also plays the piano at Mass.

"I don't think I've met her husband. What's his name?"

"Patrick, and he's usually hiding in the back, doing the books. A good, solid man he is. Dependable to a fault. If he found a wallet full of cash on the ground, he'd turn it in without a thought."

I wrinkled my nose. "You don't find many folks like that in Miami, let me tell you. Or at least, there are so many of the other type, they're drowned out."

He took a sip of his tea and paused. The silence had just about grown uncomfortable when he spoke in a quiet voice, almost with awe. "I've been to New York City once, for an ecumenical conference. Not even seminary in Glasgow prepared me for that experience."

"New York is not for the faint of heart or the meek of soul, that's for certain. The biggest difference with Miami is that we spread out rather than up. And the ocean is cleaner."

The silence grew again. I was already halfway through with my tea, and I'd run out of small talk. He was going to ask me to Mass. That's what small town priests did, right? And I wanted to refuse him, but how could I do so and not lose face in this new town? If there were ten non-Catholics, I'd be surprised, from what Gran had said.

Father Fraser drank the last of his tea and cleared his throat. Then he rose and put out a hand. "Well, I've taken enough of your time, Skye. I do welcome you to Ballybás. I would love to see you at Mass this Sunday."

I took it, plastered a smile on my face, and said, "Of course. I look forward to it."

After Father Fraser left, I let out a long-suffering sigh and locked the door. I was about peopled out by now and needed some time alone to recharge.

I also wanted to find out where those darned keys fit.

Clenching my jaw with determination, I grabbed the keys from their hook and went to the kitchen door. Nope. Then the door from the parlour into the pub. Nope.

I tried the bathroom downstairs and then climbed to the second floor. No luck on that bathroom, either. Then I tried each of the bedrooms, with the master bedroom last.

After each one resulted in failure, I sat on the bed, staring at the antique keys. Did Gran have an attic? I hadn't seen another door, but now my eyes drifted to the ceiling. Walking out into the hall, I spied the panel in the ceiling that usually indicated attic space. How could I reach it? The ceiling was at least seven feet high.

Downstairs again, I searched through the utility closet for a stepladder, but came up empty. Out in the garden, I looked in the first shed, then the second. Piled under some garden implements, I found an old but sturdy step-ladder with four steps.

"Aha!" Triumphantly, I went back inside and upstairs. Perched on the top step, carefully, I stared at the hatch. There was a keyhole, but none of the keys fit.

"Sheep nuggets." I scowled at the keys, then I pulled the hatch to the attic, and it opened easily. If I couldn't find where the keys worked, at least I could explore the hidden treasures of the attic.

After scraping my knuckles on the floorboards, I dragged myself up into the space, albeit with some grunting and kicking. Once inside, I did a slow turn, taking it all in, sneezing twice from the musty odor and dust. Sunlight crept in from chinks in the boards and the dormer windows on each end.

There must be a hundred bins, boxes, and bags up here! It would take months, maybe even years, to go through it all.

I had no idea where to start. I didn't even know if I had the energy. Okay, maybe I'd look at one box. I started a game of Which One Will I Choose. My finger didn't fall on a box, but an old vanity. The flowery decorations were very art nouveau, and I imagined that, underneath the dust and the scuffed edges, there was a beautiful piece of antique furniture hiding.

For a moment, I shut my eyes and pictured Gran as a young woman, sitting in front of the vanity, putting on make-up before a night out, and I grinned. She grinned back at me and gave me a saucy wink.

Chuckling at my silliness, I blew on the surface, and a cloud of dust billowed up. After a few coughs, I pulled open the top left drawer and found a few pairs of old leather gloves, a pair of glasses with frames pointed on the upper outside corners, and a string of pearls. I eyed the latter, but they looked like cheap knock-offs, rather than something valuable.

The bottom left drawer held silk handkerchiefs with SOS embroidered in one corner. Was that Gran, or her husband's? His name also started with S, right? Seán, I think.

Grandpa had died long before I was born, so I'd never met him. Silk handkerchiefs were before my time, but I always thought men carried them, not women.

I couldn't even remember what Grandpa had done for a living. Maybe he worked the farm? It wasn't a large one, but sufficient for a couple, I thought.

Then I pulled open the top right drawer, and had to stop and stare. The most beautiful book nestled inside, half-wrapped by a piece of white fabric. Carefully, I pulled it out.

The cover was tooled leather with swirling Celtic knotwork and several inset crystals of various colors. The purple might be amethyst, and perhaps garnet for the red. I didn't know a lot about crystals, so couldn't identify the rest, especially not in the dim attic.

Gingerly opening the cover, I touched the first blank page. Thick, cream paper with an almost rough surface. The next page held handwriting, and I recognized it instantly.

This must be Gran's diary.

CHAPTER NINE

Without even looking in the next drawer, I clutched the treasured journal to my chest and closed my eyes.

"Thank you, Gran."

You're welcome, child. A twinkle of music came with her words.

Of course, I didn't hear the words out loud. That would be nonsense. I'd never talked to Gran much, because she hated phone calls. Nonetheless, it seemed like she answered me from wherever she was now, and that made me joyful.

I tried to picture her writing on the pages, dressed in an old-fashioned nightie, the bedside lamp barely giving off enough light for her to see the ink. I started a diary a few times, but never had the gumption or determination to make more than three or four entries before forgetting.

Clutching the precious book, I climbed down from the attic hatch. Or at least, I tried to. My foot couldn't find the top step of the ladder, no matter how much I wiggled around.

I pulled up a little to peek down and orient myself. I was at least a half a foot too far to the right, so I repositioned and tried again. The ladder wobbled as I took the first step, then settled with the second, and I used the wall to brace myself.

Once on Terra Firma, or at least Hallway Firma, I hurried down to the parlour. I wanted to relish this delightful glimpse into Gran's mind and life with no distractions.

Dear Diary:

I know that's terribly trite, but sometimes it's the only proper thing to do. After all, this is for me and for you and no one else. Who cares how I write?

Today was the first day of my life after Seán. I didn't handle it particularly well. In fact, I was a right mess once everyone left after the wake. I kept a brave enough face for the punters, but I just wanted them all to go away and leave me alone. They were just here to offer sympathy. I was being churlish and selfish.

But they are gone now, and I wanted to start our relationship off with a bang.

Saoirse, 1st April

Oh, wow. This was going to be some heavy reading, no doubt about it. I couldn't digest a lot more intense entries, so I just flipped randomly through the pages. I wondered what year these entries were, but only found the day and month next to each signature.

I stopped when I spied a sketch of a fearsome creature. Some sort of howling ghost. The sketch was pretty good. The screeching face made me wobbly.

Next to it, in Gran's handwriting, was:

Ban sídhe/banshee. Spirit wails in the night at an impending death. Usually attached to a particular family. No sightings this year.

This year? Does that mean Gran had seen a Bean Sídhe in a prior year? Was she some sort of psychic, then? I flipped through some more, looking specifically for sketches.

I stopped at an enormous black cat and narrowed my eyes. The description was simply *Cat Sídhe.* The simple drawing looked suspiciously like Faelan.

Another few pages, and I came across a second sketch, this time of a gorgeous woman with black hair and blood dripping from wicked fangs. That had to be the Dearg-Due that Adanna was describing.

Sure enough, Gran had written *Dearg-Due* next to it, adding that it particularly hunted people who acted cruelly. It also favored families.

How much had Adanna and my Gran swapped stories about supernatural creatures? They seemed to like the same ones.

As I browsed further in, I stopped at a sketch of a crypt or mausoleum. A majestic construction with a stone arch, and a pointed roof. More Celtic knotwork decorated the massive door. The caption read *O'Shea Family Crypt,* and this time the shudder ran straight down my spine.

Is that where Gran is now?

Goosebumps rose on my arms, an unspoken premonition lingering. The blood-sucking fairy creature she wrote about seemed to be more than just words on a page.

At that moment, someone pounded at the door, and I nearly jumped straight out of my skin and up the attic hatch, no ladder required.

"Hold your horses! I'm coming, I'm coming." I slammed the book shut and put it on the side table.

More pounding, and it was coming from the pub door. My ire was growing with each step and as soon as I unlocked the latch, I flung the door wide. "What?!"

An older man with a paunch, dark hair brushed to one side, and a scowl stood in my pub's doorway. He spoke in an imperious tone. "Are you Skye O'Shea?"

Crossing my arms, I wanted to retreat from this angry man, but I forced myself to stand firm. "Who's asking?"

He lifted his chin. The buttons across his belly strained, and I hoped they wouldn't pop into my face. "I'm Cormac O'Leary."

He reminded me of every privileged white male who thought women's only place was in the kitchen, barefoot and pregnant. I had no evidence to back up this impression, other than his attitude, but I already hated him. "Oh, yeah. I heard about you. You own the other pub. So, are you the welcoming committee? If so, you're already too late. Adanna showed me around."

I started shutting the door again, but O'Leary shot his arm out and stopped it. "Are you opening this pub again?"

Raising my eyebrows, I asked, "I have no obligation to inform you of my plans."

His scowl deepened, and his cheeks and nose turned red. "You think you can make this a go, do you? An American woman, running an Irish pub?"

Well, now I'd *have* to make it a go, just to prove this jerk wrong. I matched his scowl. "We'll see, won't we?"

A sly smile spread across his face. "Heard you had a spot of trouble last night. An unexpected visitor, was it? A woman living alone has to be careful, doesn't she?"

Ice shot down my spine, as that was Armand's favorite phrase, once I asked him for a divorce. "Is that a threat?"

"I don't make threats, girl."

Now, he was pissing me off. "I am *not* your girl!"

He let out a nasty laugh. Armand used that sort of laugh on me. "Your grandmother barely kept this place alive, and she was a local. No one's going to come to your place when they've got a proper pub to go to. Take my advice, girl. Go back home to your place. Or someone might just take this all away from you!"

I pressed my lips together, then said, "This *is* my place. This is where my family lived for generations. My blood is soaked into the very earth here. I won't be frightened off by any bully!"

I slammed the door shut, drowning out O'Leary's mocking laughter. My hands trembled as I forced them to unclench. The encounter left a lingering unease, a clash of wills that would undoubtedly surface again.

Once O'Leary was gone, I sat heavily into one of the chairs in the pub, a mismatched one near a round table. All energy drained from my body from that encounter, but I was proud of myself. I held my own, I didn't burst into tears in front of him, and I didn't cower.

I might cry now, though, now that no one could see. Tears burned behind my eyes, and I let them come.

By everything holy, will I ever be free from men like that? Men who thought they could just push around anyone they wanted to. Men who tried to dominate, so full of testosterone poisoning, they ought to keel over at any moment.

But they didn't. It was up to strong women to teach them better. Gran had been a strong woman. Even my mother had been strong, until cancer destroyed her. I had never been strong, but I wanted to be.

I clenched my jaw to keep another wave of tears at bay. This is what Gran would have wanted from me. To stand my ground and be independent. Why else would she have gifted me the pub and B&B? I would have to do her proud, to walk in her footsteps.

After only a few more minutes of wallowing, I grabbed a napkin, blew my nose, and stood again. I had things to do if I was going to open this place.

Armed with a notepad and pencil, I toured the main pub, jotting down tasks. Those flickering fluorescent lights needed attention, annoyingly enough.

There were six small, round tables, each one with two or three chairs. Very few of them matched, but they were all dark wood and oozed old world charm. Dark wood panel walls would be lit from the windows during the daytime, when they weren't boarded over. One window was cracked, but the rest looked sound enough.

Then I moved to the bar. This was a long, solid piece with stools surrounding the outside, taps in two places inside, and a wall covered in a mirror and shelves of liquor bottles behind it. A small stand might hold chips or other snacks on the end near the front door. The other end had a door to a single toilet.

A wooden stool with a cracked back caught my eye, and another wobbled precariously. The taps seemed in desperate need of some tender care. I'd have to contact suppliers for kegs, bottles, snacks, and cleaning things.

Definitely lots of cleaning things. The place was musty and smelled of smoke and stale beer. I wrinkled my nose and added air fresheners and bleach to the list.

I'd have to figure out if I could run the place myself. I doubted it, so I'd check out if any local girls wanted a job. I didn't want to risk those rough boys helping out. A prejudice, certainly, but until I knew people around here better, I was safer with female help.

One drawer behind the bar was stuck. I needed to see what Gran already had before I could make a list of what we lacked, so I searched for a toolbox. Nothing in the pub, the pub kitchen room, nor the actual kitchen.

After trying a few closets, I found a dusty toolbox. Hefting it, I grunted. The thing was heavier than I thought! Armand had always taken care of repairs, or called a repairman if he couldn't fix it, so I had very little experience at such things.

I found a flathead screwdriver and tried to pry the drawer open. I got it open about an inch, but it wouldn't budge further.

After running back to the kitchen, I grabbed the bar of soap, then ran it along the edges of the drawer. That didn't quite work as I expected.

I tugged and tugged, pulling at it with all my weight. Suddenly, the whole thing slipped free, and I fell on my backside. "Oof!"

Staring at the empty drawer, I laughed at myself. All that effort for no reward. At least the rubber mat cushioned my fall. I'd still be sporting one heck of a bruise on my backside.

Gingerly, I rose again, and ruefully shoved the empty drawer back home. I'd made enough notes in the pub and so I moved to the pub kitchen.

While there had been a stock of liquor bottles in the bar, though covered with dust, the little kitchen was almost bare. A fridge for sandwich makings, perhaps. Cabinets with plates, cups, and silverware. A sink and a chopping board.

Where did she keep the actual kegs and bottles? I glanced around, and then went back into the pub. Then I spied a hatch in the floor, near the end of the pub. "Aha!"

I lifted it up and eyed the steep wooden plank stairs. The dank smell made me put off going down there. "Maybe another day." However, I left it open so the basement space could vent that damp. Besides, I'd had enough with dark places for a while.

Next, I went into the main house. There were things that needed fixing here, too. I still hadn't decided if I wanted to open the B&B portion of Gran's business. Maybe one thing at a time.

A hallway light needed a new bulb. The downstairs bathroom door handle was loose. Maybe I could fix that one myself.

I fetched the toolbox again, fishing out a Philips-head screwdriver, and knelt next to the door. I tightened the screws and tested the knob.

It fell off in my hand. Staring at it with my mouth open, I probably looked like… what was the word Gran used? An *amádan*, that's what it was. A silly person.

Gripping the knob, I pressed my lips together and peered through the hole it had fallen from. My mind just wouldn't work to figure out how to fix it.

Fine. First, I'd make a list of repairs that were beyond my ability. That would likely be a long one. In the meantime, I needed to take stock of the garden and what was needed to get that under control.

I knew next to nothing about gardening. Most of my life had been in apartments, so I had no flower beds or herb gardens. I was no gourmet chef, either. I was perfectly happy with a microwaved meal, soup, or sandwich. Which meant I had no interest in growing fresh fruits and vegetables up until now.

As I opened the door, Faelan darted past me. "Faelan! Stop doing that! If you trip me and I die, you won't get fed anymore! Do you hear me?"

The cat had disappeared before I stopped talking. *Darn fairy cat.*

Outside, I stared across the backyard with my hands on my hips. Two sheds and an open shelter. Food garden, flower garden, herb garden. Or did they call them kitchen gardens? No matter. It was wild and overgrown, and probably full of weeds, choking the useful plants out of existence.

I would probably have to leave the garden for next year. This wild mess was too much for me to get my mind around at the moment. Then I wondered if someone in town would be willing to work on it for me.

Or if I could even afford to hire another person. If I had to pay for a barmaid, likely not.

Ugh. That meant I'd have to start figuring budgets and I hated numbers. To keep my mind off that, I went to the open shelter. That only held a few old bales of hay. *Next!*

I moved to the second shed and hesitated. This was where I'd found Brian last night. I should call it the Dead Shed. Silly name, but I needed all the giggles I could get. It helped me not think about Brian's incredibly pale face.

The police tape was all gone, so they must have finished up their investigation. Should I check with Gard McCarthy first? No, this was my garden. The tape was gone. I probably shouldn't go inside, though. I should finish my inventory.

As I was trying to make up my mind, I noticed some footprints. Not the Gard's prints, as I saw those easily enough, going back and forth from the house. Adanna had been wearing women's boots, and her prints were there. Then the ones from the driveway, which must be the coroner's.

But there were two other sets and a scuffle. One must be Brian's, but whose were the others? Surely, Gard McCarthy had seen these and taken photographs. Don't they take plasters or something of any suspicious prints?

I knelt next to them, and noticed red dirt, like the stuff under Adanna's window. The prints were thin but long. Most likely a man, but with very slender feet. Sneakers of some sort, with curly designs on them. Could they belong to the man who had been in the car when Brian hit me? The one who ran away with Cherie?

More likely, it was one of the toughs who gave me a hard time. Heck, it could be O'Leary, the toad who was trying to bully me away from my Gran's home. Or someone else I'd never met.

I should leave the policing to the police. Gard McCarthy kept brushing aside my suggestions, so obviously didn't think he needed help. He probably didn't. He knew this town a whole lot better than I did.

Faelan rushed by me with a growl, and I fell backwards, my butt hitting a flagstone. "Oof! Cat! You're using up your nine lives one by one, you know!"

I got to my feet again, carefully. My butt would definitely be a collage of bruises by tomorrow. The black cat zipped toward the house and through his little cat door. I followed, intent upon finding out what, precisely, his problem was. If he was a talking cat, I meant to make him start talking.

Make him sing like a bird. I giggled at the irony of that line for a cat, despite its cheesiness.

However, once I got inside, I heard a sound outside again. Had Faelan flanked me? He must be magic. But no, it wasn't a cat. It was Adanna, staring at the ground near the Dead Shed. What was she doing here?

I was about to open the door when she glanced around and hurried off, as if caught doing something illegal. *What in the name of all that's holy was going on here?*

I wanted to follow, but something in the back of my mind said to stay put. No real words, just a general feeling of *don't go.*

What was going on with me? Voices and music and unexplained notions. Had I entered *The Twilight Zone?*

Maybe Gran had written something in her diary. Or that darned cat would know.

"Faelan! Faelan, where did you get to? I need to ask you some things."

Running paws upstairs. I pelted up and then regretted it when I got to the top. My body was still complaining from the abuse I'd been putting it through. "Faelan? Where are you?"

I peeked into each of the empty guest rooms. The Sage Room, Periwinkle Room, and Rose Room. As if this was some grand country house. Shall we sup in the larger dining room this evening, Mum?

A streak of black flew down the stairs. "Faelan! Get back here!"

I almost slid down the stairs, which my backside would have raised quite a fuss over, when the flapping of the cat door heralded Faelan's exit.

Well, he had to come in sometime to eat, didn't he? I'd get him then.

Or at least, that's what I thought. However, a dozen shakes of the cat food bag didn't work. Even resorting to running the can opener revealed no maddening black cat.

Giving it up as a lost cause, I heated a can of soup, grabbed a spoon, and curled up in the comfy chair, with Gran's diary. I treasured this glimpse into her thoughts, a precious gift I would savor for a long time.

I reread some of the entries about supernatural creatures, and then went back to the beginning. I imagined I heard a faint tune as I opened the decorated cover.

Dear Diary:

Burying Seán was harder than I thought it would be. We had loved each other for decades, but the last few years had turned almost perfunctory. We were more like comfortable roommates than a married couple.

But I mourned him properly, laid him to rest, and put on a proper wake. The neighbors all came and cried their tears. Many brought me food. I'm swimming in pies. How will I ever eat these all? I wish my daughter was still here, but she followed that Yank.

I never liked that man. George is the brutal sort. He won't even marry her. He just wants to milk his cow without buying it, the selfish cad. Well, perhaps Maeve will come to her senses soon. I can but hope.

Pray? No, I don't pray. I gave up on that sort of thing years ago. There, I put it in writing. I can't tell anyone, not here in Ireland.

Certainly not in the country. But I cannot believe in a God who lets such cruelty fall upon innocent children. So, I kicked that habit. Get it? Habit? Nuns? Well, I never expected a diary to actually laugh, anyway.

The diary might not laugh at her puns, but I did. I'd only heard her voice a few times since I was a kid, but as I read her words, written in her handwriting, I heard her voice as if she was right behind me, reciting it as my eyes scanned the page.

Sheepishly, I glanced around, just in case she *was* creeping up behind me. This was her house, after all. If she was going to hang around and haunt a place, this would be it.

Or a weird old clock in Dublin airport. I shivered. Had that been Gran? Or just my wild sleep-deprived imagination?

I let out a mighty yawn and closed the diary. I would enjoy consuming this in tiny bites. It would give me a chance to get to know Gran. I already felt like I knew her far more than I'd known my mother.

Placing the precious diary on the side table, I rinsed out my bowl and placed it on the drying rack. Gran had no dishwasher and really, why would I need one? I was living alone, and had no husband to use every dish in the sink while he was cooking up some obscure delicacy.

Sure, I missed his cooking. I was a horrible cook, but I was happy with simple meals. I did *not* miss cleaning up after Armand.

Of course, if I opened the pub, that would be much more cleaning, unless I hired someone. If I did hire someone, they'd need to be strong enough to wrestle a keg down those narrow pub stairs.

With a sigh and a tall stretch of my hands, I plodded up the stairs. The hour had grown late, and today had been full of things. I was dead tired.

After I dressed in my pajamas–green with shamrocks on it, pure tourist tat–I crawled into the huge bed and closed my eyes.

I must have fallen right asleep, because it only seemed minutes later that I woke with a start. I squinted at the clock, which was the old-fashioned analog kind with arms rather than a digital display. Three in the morning. What woke me?

The night air held an eerie stillness, until a sudden crash echoed from downstairs, accompanied by that odd melody.

What, was someone murdering a piano in my house? Or maybe Adanna had returned, and let herself in? That wasn't kosher at all, even for a new friend.

I seized the phone from my bedside, and flipped on the flashlight app. Then, I grabbed the closest weapon I could find, an old cane in the corner. Had this been Gran's?

Thus armed, I crept down the hall, unsure of what awaited in the darkness.

My butt bruises hurt as I climbed down the stairs. I wasn't used to all these stair-climbings. Houses in Florida tended to be single-story.

I searched each room of the house but found nothing amiss. Not one thing out of place. I flashed the phone light out the windows, as well, but nothing stirred in the garden, even the wind. I let out a breath of relief. I hadn't wanted to find another body.

Wearily, I climbed back upstairs, put the cane back, and wriggled back under the covers. Just as I settled back into bed, Faelan leapt on my chest.

"You! Where have you been?"

Faelen kneaded my belly, then settled down with his butt in my face.

"Oh, so now you won't talk?" He just twitched his tail. "Seriously, cat? Move your butt, please. I don't want whatever you left in the sand on my nose."

He moved slightly over, but purred so loud, it sounded like a motorcycle. Despite my annoyance, his purrs soothed me, and soon I was drifting back asleep.

An image of Brian's incredibly pale face flashed before me. As I fell again into dreams, the magical monster chased us both through endless bogs, screaming as it flew.

CHAPTER TEN

When I finally clawed my way out of slumber the next morning, Faelan was still purring on my chest like an outboard motor. He must have been there all night.

Faelan woke with slow stretches and padded away without a care in the world. I had a care, and it had to do with getting to the bathroom in time before my bladder burst.

Once my morning ablutions were complete, I dressed and went downstairs to make some coffee.

Or maybe I should start having tea each morning?

It seemed like a more Irish thing to do. After all, I was pretending to be a local, so I had to add all the expected stereotypes and trappings, if I wanted to be accepted as such.

I'd never truly be accepted as a local, but I had to try. For my own sake, as well as Gran's legacy. I'd also made a promise to be true to myself, right? Somehow, I had to try to do both. This was a good time to start.

As I sipped my tea, mellowed with plenty of milk, I gazed outside. The May morning was still chilly and fog clung to the garden, obscuring anything beyond it. No traffic yet. Then I tried to remember what day it was. Friday? I thought so. I wondered if the weekend would bring more visitors.

May was what Gran called 'shoulder season' in Ireland. High season was June, July, and August, but more and more people were visiting in May and September. Airfare was cheaper, the days were still pretty long, and the weather was fair enough, if a bit nippy in the mornings. The crowds were thinner, at least before the pandemic. Now, people were surging back to their long-missed holidays, and lots of places felt that impact. Those which had survived, at least.

Gran had mentioned another pub which had gone under during that time. Along with several restaurants and shops. Not just here in Ballybás, but all over Ireland. A sad time, she said, but it also meant there was less competition for the surviving establishments.

I finished off my tea and decided I wanted to walk in the garden, despite the chill. I needed to get over my fear of the Dead Shed.

Pulling on a green wool shawl from Gran's things, I stepped outside. The humidity was stronger than in Miami, but so much cooler, it didn't feel oppressive at all. At least, to me. Maybe the locals had a different opinion.

Another way in which I wasn't a local.

I strolled down the path past the kitchen garden, noting a few butterflies who must have been up with the dawn, and a lonely bee buzzing around, which made me give a sad smile. I mourned the loss of my collection. I used to have a notebook with bees and a few t-shirts with silly bee slogans, like 'Bee yourself' and 'Bee strong!'

As I neared the Dead Shed, I balked at going inside just yet. Instead, I walked around the back. I hadn't explored the surrounding area. The path led around the wooden building and then to a longer trail along the property line.

Something glinted, which caught me by surprise. In this fog? The sun was nowhere to be found. I crouched down, trying to spy it again, and spotted a long, thin piece of metal, bent in an L-shape.

I didn't touch it. Even if the police *had* cleared it, I shouldn't mess with new evidence. A bit of white paper was under it, and I craned my neck to see what it was.

O'Leary's Pub. Black letters in a vaguely Celtic-style font, with three stylized shamrocks and a glass of Guinness. The business card looked a bit worse for wear, with dark brown stains. That could be dirt, but I suspected it was dried blood. Again, I didn't dare touch it. Maybe it was coffee?

Something just didn't make sense. Those two young people who were in Brian's car must have had something to do with this. I just didn't have any proof, so the Gard had dismissed my notion out of hand.

Was it just being disdained that rankled me? Maybe I was making things up to feel relevant in this new place. No, that's what Armand had always accused me of, whenever I tried to speak up for myself. I refused to let his opinions color my new life.

Right, back to the murder. As a nurse, I'd seen plenty of death, including murders. Sure, none of them had intimately involved me, but still, why would this one haunt me?

Brian's pale face peered into my memory, and I grasped onto that clue. Especially after overhearing Gard McCarthy talking to the coroner about all his blood being drained.

So, what could drain his blood? A syringe, of course, but other equipment was needed. Equipment one might find in an embalmer's office. Most people weren't carrying around arterial tubes and chemical injectors in their back pockets.

Then my mind wandered back to Gran's diary and Adanna's tales. The Dearg-Due could drain blood. Gran had written the details of how one was formed. Usually, a woman was killed under tragic circumstances. A broken heart or the betrayal of a true love, something of that sort.

But even if some supernatural creature was at work here, that meant someone else had been killed. We only had one body.

I stared at the O'Leary's card again, half-buried in the dirt outside of the Dead Shed. Then I remembered that Adanna mentioned she'd seen Brian and a woman at O'Leary's the night before he was killed. I wondered if anyone had seen the woman who was in his car lately. What was her name? Cherie. Or even the other man with them, the one she called Gerald.

Well, I could ask around about her.

If Cormac O'Leary decided to get nasty about things, he could do so in full view of everyone else in his pub. Most bullies preferred to have no audience for their anger. I was counting on that.

In a flash of inspiration, I snapped a zoomed-in pic of the business card and bit of bent metal, then I backed up and took another shot at normal distance. The shed was identifiable, but I could still see the card nestled in the brush. A third photo of the shed in my yard, with the pub/house behind it.

Armed with this evidence, I stalked over to O'Leary's.

It was dark and closed. Right. It was still only about ten in the morning, and the pub wouldn't be open yet. Even if he served food, which I had no idea about, he likely wouldn't open his doors until eleven at the earliest.

My stomach rumbled, and reminded me that I'd only had a measly cup of tea for breakfast. I was used to a more substantial morning meal. Of course, that had been when I was working a full shift at the hospital. In the months since my hasty departure, I'd fallen into a rather lazy morning habit. It was lovely to wake when I wanted to and get enough sleep for the first time since I started college.

But now, the hunger was upon me, as Gran used to say. I remembered seeing a breakfast café along one of the side streets, and I was eager to meet more people, so I searched for it.

The butcher's shop was across the street, but I wasn't exactly in the mood for raw meat. A craft shop, a shoe store. *Oh, a bookstore!* I'd have to check that out later.

Next was a woolen shop, then a fish-n-chips place. There, just past the clinic, was another cross street, and this one had an open café. Score!

Hesitantly, I entered the Blarney Scones café. I loved the punny name. The heart-warming aroma of baking bread and fresh-brewed coffee caressed my nose. Small tables lined one side of the narrow restaurant, while a counter lined the right, with glass cases for pastries and sweets.

The wall had a few posters and tchotchkes. One had a bee, with the words "If you can't bee good, bee kind," and it made me grin.

Several coffee machines behind the counter promised me some good coffee. At least, I hoped. The tea was lovely, but it wasn't enough. I would have to acclimate myself to the new habit.

A youngish man with a long, dark ponytail put on a huge smile. "*Dia duit.* You're the new girl, are ye? Saoirse's lass? I'm Joshua."

"Yes, I'm Skye. Pleased to meet you."

"Welcome to Ballybás! Are you after some breakfast? Or an early lunch, if you like."

"Coffee. A very large coffee." I glanced at the chalkboard menu behind him. I shouldn't gorge myself, but I was *really* hungry. I could afford to splurge a bit. "You have a full Irish breakfast?"

His grin got even deeper, if that was possible. "That we do. You want everything? Black pudding, mushrooms, beans, all that?"

I wrinkled my nose. "Leave off the beans, please."

Joshua let out a chuckle. "Brilliant. Have a seat and I'll bring everything to you."

I sat in a chair facing the plate glass windows and let out a breath. This seemed so achingly normal, and yet still so strange. I was in Ireland. Living in a small town. One where everyone already seemed to know my face.

An older man with a flat cap and a tweed jacket walked by, halted for a moment, frowned at me, and hurried past.

Miami was anonymous. There was safety in anonymity. For some reason, I felt exposed here, as if people saw me naked. They probably knew my Gran far better than I ever had. And I was trying to take over her place. To fit into her shoes. My Gran, who I only knew through letters, while the whole town knew her much better.

Joshua placed a steaming mug in front of me, and the aroma comforted my soul. "Here's your coffee. There's a sidebar there with your milk and sugar and the like."

The sidebar wasn't like Starbucks, but more extensive than I'd imagined for Ireland. All types of fake sugar sachets, real sugar, even brown sugar. Several additive flavors. Maybe Ireland wasn't so ignorant of proper coffee culture, after all.

After adding a splash of vanilla flavor and a sachet of sugar, I sat again and watched the street as I sipped my morning brew. Only a few people were out and about at this time of day. Wait, what was today? Friday. Most folks would be at work already. Tomorrow, everything might look different, especially since this village was on the tourist path. Gran had always complained about the influx of tourists, despite the fact that she made a great deal of profit from their visits.

As Joshua placed an enormous plate in front of me, covered in fried deliciousness, I took a deep breath, savoring the bacon, eggs, sausage, everything terrible for me. But so delicious. While I couldn't eat a Full Irish every day, I was still in honeymoon mode here. I doubted the locals ate breakfasts like this.

And I wasn't a local, not yet. Doubt crept over me, that I'd ever be able to make this place feel like home.

That woman with the red-blond hair and glasses I'd seen the other day walked by, again exuding that yellow aura. Sunny and friendly, like someone I'd want to know. If she came into the café, I'd ask her to join me. But no, she kept walking, intent on her errands.

I took alternating bites of eggs, toast, and sausage. Soon, I was halfway done, and felt full to bursting.

Then that gang of young men walked by. I noted their outfits, not too different from the self-styled rebels of my youth. Boys with too much time and not enough sense. Usually, they grew up and gained some of the latter. Or they ended up in jail or worse. Miami was a rough place to grow up unless you were rich.

One of the boys glanced into the window, and I leaned back, just out of sight. I don't know why I was so afraid of them. They were just a bunch of kids. They *had* thumped my car and that had triggered a panic attack. I had no wish to have another one today.

Then Cormac O'Leary marched past, and I hastily tossed the last few sips of my coffee back, left cash on the table for Joshua, and hurried out.

I had to jog to catch the other pub owner. As I grew near, he turned around, staring at me with wide eyes. "Miss O'Shea! You're running like the devil was after you. How can I help you?"

I must have been flushed, and my cheeks were warm. I'd expected him to growl angrily, but he spoke in a reasonable tone, almost concerned. He didn't smile, but at least he didn't scowl like before.

But if he was willing to act friendly, I wasn't going to look a gift horse in the mouth, even if it meant confronting him alone. I kept my tone light. "I'm trying to puzzle something out and would like your help. Can we go somewhere to talk for a few minutes?"

Several emotions flashed across his face as he processed this request, and his eyes darted back and forth before he broke out into a very plastic grin that didn't come close to reaching his eyes. "Of course. Come into the pub, and I'd be glad to help you in any way I can."

Yeah, right. I'd met enough narcissistic scum to know fake charm when I saw it. Still, it might help me get some information.

By that time, we'd reached his pub. He glanced around before unlocking the door, and then pushed it open as a bell jingled. He waved me in with a gallant half-bow. I wasn't buying it in the slightest but walked in with a gracious nod of thanks.

This bar screamed *glitz.* Dark mahogany everything– the walls, the bar, the matching tables and chairs. Even the barstools were wood, with red velvet pads on the seats. Stained glass windows reminiscent of 19th century San Francisco let in a rainbow of morning light. Ceiling tiles were carved in art deco designs which matched the cabinets and dividers between the tables.

An enormous deer head trophy was on the wall behind the bar, in the middle of the mirrored wall. Expensive bottles of alcohol at the top, including some brands of whiskey I was certain were hundreds of dollars each.

There was even a crystal chandelier in the ceiling. The tourists probably ate this stuff up!

And yet, for all the glamor, it had no charm. Gran's place was simple and plain but felt homey and comfortable. This place was a Hollywood producer's idea of what Irish pubs should be.

O'Leary pulled out a chair for me at one of the tables. "Have a seat, Miss O'Shea. Can I get you a pint?"

I narrowed my eyes. "It's a bit early for me. Could I have some ice water?"

Maybe I could get the satisfaction of throwing it in his lying face.

"Ice water, coming up." He flashed me another smile filled with fake charm and went behind the bar. When he returned, he carried a tumbler of water for me with one grudging ice cube, and a glass of whiskey for himself, no ice.

He sat down, took a sip of his drink, and then folded his hands. "Now. To what do I owe the pleasure of your company on this fine morning?"

I cleared my throat, suddenly nervous. We were alone in his pub and no one else knew I was there. He'd already been aggressive and angry at me before. Why did I get myself into this situation, again? Oh, right. To help someone who was killed. Someone else who had been aggressive and angry at me.

"I'm searching for some people I met a few days ago. I was hoping you'd remember them."

The older man cocked his head, his smile not changing in the slightest. "What did these people look like?"

With a swallow, I said, "The woman's name is Cherie. She's tall and thin. Like, very thin. She has a round face, with straight black hair almost to her waist. Perhaps about thirty years old, give or take. I don't know the man's name, but he was lanky, with blond hair."

O'Leary's eyes had widened slightly at the description, but he just tapped his chin as he gazed up to the left. "Hmm, let me think about that. A few nights ago, you say? So, maybe Wednesday?"

He recognized her, all right. I'd seen plenty of patients and could tell when someone knew something but was trying to hide it.

I counted the days back to the accident. I arrived in town on Wednesday. Had it only been two days ago? It felt like two weeks. "Tuesday, more likely. She might have been in with a young man, also very thin, but with blond, wispy hair."

The pub owner pressed his lips tight, then shook his head. "No, no I don't think so. He doesn't sound familiar at all. There are so many people coming through here, I don't even see them all on a busy night. I have staff, you know."

He gave me another smarmy smile. I returned it. "Understood. I didn't think you'd know everything that went on in your establishment. Thank you for your time."

I rose to leave, but he grabbed my hand. Panic bubbled up from my stomach into my throat. "Wait, why did you think she was here at my pub?"

Did I want to mention the card? That was one of my few clues, and I needed to know if there was any connection, but I worried about his reaction. Still, I had to find courage somehow. Tamping down my fear, I replied, "You heard about the dead man at my farm, I know."

I studied his expression, but it didn't change at all. I gave him props for facial control, at least.

"Well, I'd seen him with these two people before. Also… I found your card at the police scene."

He let out a guffaw. "That's mostly knees. Anyone could have grabbed a card from my register over there," he gestured behind him, "and dropped it. It didn't even have to be a human."

He couldn't be talking about the banshees and Fair Folk, could he? O'Leary didn't seem the type. "What do you mean?"

With a dismissive handwave, he said, "Ah, it could have just blown around until it landed in your garden. We had a grand storm a week ago. The wind is fierce around here, or didn't you notice?"

I pressed my lips together, then said, "It was ground into the dirt, and it had blood on it."

His smile fell a notch. "Blood, you say? Are you sure, now?"

I glanced away. "No, not a hundred percent sure. However, I've seen enough blood to recognize it on sight, even dried on paper."

He gripped my shoulder, and panic rose in my throat. I tried to wrench it away, but his fingers dug painfully into my muscle. "Oh, you have, have you? That's an interesting thing, so it is."

His condescension was turning my panic into anger, and I needed to get out of there before I did something stupid. Like kicking him in the nether regions. Hard. "I am a nurse. Of course, I've seen blood. Now, if you will let go of my arm, I'll leave you to your day. Thank you for your help."

As if he'd been any help at all.

He gave my arm a warning shake, but did let go. "Now, now, don't go rushing off, girl. As it happens, perhaps I *do* know something about your dead man, at least."

Speaking through clenched teeth, my arm ached as I growled, "He's not my dead man."

"Ah, well, of course not." The fake smile was even wider now. "You don't have a man, from what I hear. Well, as I was saying, I *did* see your dead man." He paused to gauge my reaction to him repeating that phrase. I didn't give him the satisfaction and kept my expression frozen.

"You did? When?"

"On Wednesday night, as it happens. After your rather spectacular entrance into town."

I narrowed my eyes at this. "Spectacular?"

"You certainly made sure everyone noticed your arrival, so you did." He placed a finger on the side of his nose, as if he was sharing a secret that I should keep silent about. *As if.* "So, back to your man. He was having a rather intense discussion with one of our local lads."

Despite myself, that caught my interest. "Local lad? Who?"

"The hipster. You met him, aye? Helped you with your car?"

I blinked a few times. "Seán? He had an argument with Seán?" First impressions can be misleading, but I'd definitely gotten a kind vibe from him. Was I so wrong?

O'Leary gave a casual shrug. "Not truly an argument. I said *intense discussion*, did I not? Seán tries not to let his temper get the better of him. He's gotten into trouble for that in the past."

That sounded ominous. "Oh? How so?"

With a self-satisfied smirk, he said, "You'll have to ask him about all that. If you're here long enough, that is. Not my tale to tell, to be sure."

I sat back down, my hands on the table, and leaned forward. "So, then, what was this *'intense discussion'* about?"

With a chuckle, he leaned back and crossed his arms. "I couldn't possibly say. It was crowded that night, like most nights. No one could hear a donkey's bellow in that ruckus."

Before I could ask how angry they looked, the door jingled, and I spun to see who it was. A young woman wearing a white shirt and short, black skirt strode in, nodded to O'Leary, and went through the bar, into the next room without a word.

The man rose. "My staff are beginning to arrive, so I'll bid you farewell."

I got to my feet as well and turned toward the door.

"Miss O'Shea? Do me a favor, will you?"

I turned back, apprehension rising again.

"Be careful. You're playing with some dangerous matches."

As I stepped out into the brisk May air, a shadow moved at the corner of my vision. I turned, but there was no one there. A cold tremor swept through me, a feeling that I was being watched.

CHAPTER ELEVEN

As I stood outside McCarthy's pub, everything whirled in my head, and I couldn't catch any of the facts long enough to sort them into any order. I needed to get more information.

My first thought was to go to Adanna, but I couldn't get over the notion she'd been up to something in my garden. I didn't want to talk to her until I figured out her game. If she had a game. Was my paranoia getting the better of me?

My next option was to find Seán and ask him what he was arguing about with a man who was now dead.

Wait, why didn't the police do all this? Or maybe Gard McCarthy had already gone through these steps. If that was the case, I should just leave everything alone. It wasn't like I didn't have my own things to deal with. There was so much work to be done on the house and the pub, not to mention that blasted garden.

But Brian's pale face haunted my thoughts. Besides, someone had chosen to get me involved, by dumping the body in *my* shed. So, instead of turning left to go back home, I turned right and walked the block to the Gard station.

With each step, I rehearsed how to approach Gard McCarthy with the question. He already didn't like me. Interfering with his investigation wouldn't improve that impression. Advising him on how to do his job would be even worse.

But how could I determine if he possessed the same information as I did, without him arresting me, either for interfering or for being a suspect?

I definitely didn't want to start asking him questions, and get arrested by a jumpy, suspicious local Gard.

I stopped to look at the window display in a gift shop as I considered my options. I could leave an anonymous note with information about the business card and the bent stick of metal. That would lead him to O'Leary's. Still, he'd brushed off my questions about Cherie and Gerald without a thought. So, he wouldn't ask O'Leary about her. Which means he probably would consider that a dead end. Heck, for all I knew, he and O'Leary were cousins or something, and he wouldn't arrest a relative.

I didn't *know* that McCarthy would play favorites, even if he was related to a suspect. I'd heard all sorts of stories about small towns and how people looked after their own.

I couldn't risk it. The guilt haunting me wouldn't allow me to risk it.

On the other hand, what if McCarthy blew me off? At least I'd have tried. With that determination, I marched the half-block to the Gard station.

Only to find it closed. The door was locked and knocking did nothing. He must be out policing someone else. With a sigh, I sat on a bench outside.

Now what? I should call the Gard office and leave a message.

When I looked at my phone, I realized the battery was about dead and I didn't have the number. That would have to wait.

I should go find Seán and ask him about Brian. He was sure to have some sort of reasonable explanation. Or was that just my attraction to him speaking? I couldn't afford to be attracted to anyone, not yet. Maybe in a couple years, when my wounds had started healing. Not now.

I didn't even know where Seán lived or what he did for a living.

O'Leary had called him *the hipster man*. Had he meant hippie? Or an actual hipster? He'd worn comfortable, low-key clothing. A thick t-shirt with a light jacket and faded jeans. No tie-dye or Birkenstocks to be seen. Not even a peace symbol pendant, as far as I could remember.

Regardless, I didn't even know if he'd be home midday on a Friday, so I wandered back toward my house. As I passed the clinic, I glanced in, but it was dark, too. Adanna must be doing a house call. Did people even do house calls anymore? Maybe here, where some folks had no cars but were cared for by the community. Certainly not in Miami.

I passed the corner store and turned down my street, then stopped and glanced back. Surely the shopkeeper there would know Seán and where to find him. Then she'd know I was looking for him, and that would mean gossip.

You know what? I don't care anymore.

Let them gossip all they wanted. I wasn't interested in romance, so they could talk until their lips fell off. I did have an excuse to look for him, since he paid for my car to get fixed. One should repay favors, after all. I marched into the shop and grabbed a Flake bar, just so it didn't look too bizarre.

The shop owner gave me a smile. "Will that be all, dear?"

What was her name, Máiréad? Yes, that's what the priest had said. "Sure, just need a sugar boost. Do you know where I can find Seán? I wanted to repay him for the repairs he got done on my car."

Her grin almost cracked her face in half. Was I going to have to fend off matchmakers? A single woman in Ireland was in dire peril, it seemed. "Oh, to be sure. He lives on a wee farm just past the school, like. That's about three streets down the main road."

I paid for my candy bar. "I remember passing the school on my way in. Thanks!" I started to leave, then turned back. "What does he farm?"

"He grows some veg for himself, mostly, but he keeps the bees, you see."

The bees. Of course, he was the beekeeper. He must be the same one Gran had written about, the one with the weatherwise dog. I gave her a wave as I left. "Thanks!"

I munched on the Flake bar on the way back. It was chocolate, always a good thing, but that was about it. Just a thin chocolate strip wrinkled into a bar shape. Not very tasty chocolate, at least to me. Still, it was chocolate, so I finished it. I probably wouldn't buy that again, though.

By the time I reached the end of the three streets, I had waved to a dozen people I didn't know. It still felt very strange, but that's what one did in a small town, right?

As I passed the school, I tried to gauge how many students it held. The sign said Junior National School, so I assumed that was roughly the equivalent of Junior High or Middle School. So maybe three years' worth of students? They had different names for the levels, I was sure, but I had no idea what they were.

Once past the sports field, I spied a traditional thatched farmhouse in reasonably good repair. Fresh white paint on the exterior, with red paint around the windows, and wildflowers instead of lawn. I glimpsed the odd boxes in the back, so I'd found the right place.

With more courage than I normally felt, I approached the front door and was about to knock when it swung open. A very startled Seán stared at me. "Miss O'Shea!"

I know my face was already flaming, but I tried to ignore it. "Please, call me Skye. Were you on your way out?"

"Ah, it was nothing important. How can I help you?"

"I'm so sorry to barge in like this, but do you have a few moments? I need some information."

"Of course! Come here to me, and I'll put the kettle on, like." He opened the door and I entered a whole new world, redolent of peat smoke and thatch.

Okay, yes, that was cheesy, but I'd never been inside a traditional cottage before. There appeared to be just four rooms. I stood in the main entrance room or parlor or whatever it was called. To the left, there was a huge stone fireplace that almost took up the entire wall. However, there was a stove through the open door on the left. The closed door on the right of the fireplace was likely a toilet. To the right, the open door showed a chest of drawers, so that was probably the bedroom. A back door led out into the garden.

That was it, the whole house. Cozy and charming and far lovelier than the one-bedroom apartments I'd lived in.

"I'll just be a minute. Make yourself comfortable." Seán waved toward the two chairs facing the fireplace and went into the kitchen, presumably to start the kettle. I sank into the overstuffed chair. No television, not even a radio. Just the peat fire and a bookshelf stuffed with books of all types.

I couldn't help being nosy, so I read some of the titles. A few were in Irish, but most were about farming, beekeeping, with a few novels. Thrillers, for the most part, or police procedurals. Amongst those books, I spied a few crossword books, and I grinned. We had a common interest, then.

Then my gaze fell upon a silver-framed photograph. Seán and a lovely young red-haired woman. I guess he had a girlfriend? Or a wife? I touched my brown locks and frowned, my mood falling a notch. But I didn't notice any other female things around. Perhaps she was his ex?

Suddenly, a furiously barking dog appeared in the window. I frowned and peered out. He jumped again, still barking. I hid a smile as he bounced up and down several times.

Sean came back into the main room. "Ah, pay no attention to Sétanta. He's just excited to meet people, he'll do you no harm. Do you like reading, then?"

I wanted to ask if Sétanta was the weather-wise dog Gran had mentioned, but I was always happy to talk about books. "Mostly fantasy and science fiction. I do like a good historical novel, if it's a time period I like. Sétanta is an interesting name. Does it have a meaning?"

Sean let out a chuckle as he placed the tea tray on a table between the two chairs. "Sétanta is the name of one of our Irish heroes. You might recognize him as *Cú Chulainn.* One of the worst man-boys in our colorful history. And me, I'm addicted to a good scare. My life is pretty boring, so I get my kicks on the written page, I guess."

I settled into the chair and tried to figure out where to start. "So, I'm trying to puzzle some things out, and I was hoping you could help."

"Such as?"

I girded up to ask him about the dead man, but for some reason, my courage fled. Maybe it was remembering the feeling of helplessness in front of Brian's anger, which was the first time I'd met Seán. Or just not being able to confront a man, any man, yet. At least, not if I wasn't backed into a corner. Maybe I could skirt around the subject. "I was wondering if you'd seen any new folks in town, folks that might have been out at O'Leary's a few nights ago."

"O'Leary's, eh? Has anyone warned you about him yet?"

I raised my eyebrows. "Warned me?"

"He's… well, he's not one to be crossed. He can get a bit creative with his responses. Let's leave it at that. So, a few nights ago? Are you looking for Tuesday or Wednesday?"

Filing that information on O'Leary away, I replied, "I think either would work. I'm looking for a woman."

He raised his eyebrows. "A woman, is it? D'you know her name?"

Sean was peering at me in a manner that seemed like he was assuming a lot more about me than I was saying. As if I was interested in Cherie for more than just the investigation.

I'd always been much more interested in men, but at least if the town thought I was gay, they'd hold off on the matchmaking. Maybe.

"Just her first name, Cherie. She's tall, very thin, with long, black hair. Straight down her back. She was with… she was with the man who ran into me when I arrived."

He paused for a moment, staring at the fireplace. Then he said, "Ah, right. Brian. I heard about the incident in your shed."

I wasn't sure I was up to discussing the dead man yet. "But you saw the girl?"

"Sure, and I did see her Wednesday morning. All dressed in eye-blinding pink? I was with Sétanta on the beach and noticed her further down the shore. She was walking with a young man."

My excitement was growing. "What did he look like?"

"About her age. Both thin as rails, they were. He had light hair, blowing in the wind. They were having a bit of a row, it seemed. As I came closer, his face was flushed, and her eyes were red, as if she'd been crying."

That must be the guy from the car. So, they'd argued during the day, and then Brian turned up dead, drained of all blood, in my shed.

"Did you see her anywhere else?"

He shook his head. "No, wait, I did! She was with your other man, the angry one. They went to the doctor for something. They went to the clinic the evening before. She didn't go in, but he did."

Sétanta began barking furiously again, and Seán rose. "That's his alerting bark. I'll just go see what has him in such a froth. Will you wait?"

I gave a nod as he hurried out the back door. Seán's voice took on a different tone as he talked to his dog. "What are you on about, silly boy? What do you see?"

More barking, further away.

"Ah, now. That's just a rabbit. Leave it alone. Hey! No jumping. Give over, you eejit, and stop trying to get between me and my new visitor! You're a jealous hound, you are."

When he returned, he gave an apologetic smile. "He's a grand dog, especially with the few sheep I have, but a mite jumpy with other animals. This time, it was a rabbit daring to infringe upon his territory."

It didn't seem right to launch back into a discussion of Cherie and Brian. I'd gotten part of my answer, at least. I still couldn't bring myself to ask directly about Brian, though I had no idea why.

I wanted to escape now but we hadn't finished our tea yet. Instead, I glanced out the back window, searching for a different subject. "Máiréad at the corner shop told me you keep bees?"

A grin replaced his nervousness. "I do. I've been at that for years, now. I bring honey to the farmer market, and a few of the local shops."

"And you can make a living at that?"

Sean laughed out loud. "Oh, no, far from it. That's only a wee bit of my income. No, I've got residuals from my Da's books. He was an author."

"Really? What did he write?"

He waved his hand. "Nothing you know. Unless you can read the Irish?" He arched an eyebrow at me, but I shook my head.

"Well, I didn't expect you to, and you being from America. He wrote some poetry and short stories. The Gaelteacht schools picked up some of his work to teach with. They still do, so I get the royalties from that. Some family money helped."

I couldn't quite grasp the idea of just living on bits of income here and there, but I'd never had any sort of legacy of any kind from my parents, except abuse and neglect.

I stared into my tea and decided I needed to get out of there before I started baring my entire life's story to this kind man. I downed the rest of my drink and climbed to my feet. "Thank you, Seán, for the tea. I need to get going though, and I'm sure you have some work to do. You must have been heading somewhere when I arrived?"

"Sure, and I was, but nothing that couldn't bide for a while to share some time with a lovely girl."

I hurried to the door, but Seán was faster, and he held it open for me. "Will I see you around later, then?"

Outside, two older women were walking by. They spied us, and then fell to whispering. I guess I just started my own gossip.

Sean's smile was dazzling, and I hurried away from the too-bright light.

Had Adanna deliberately not mentioned seeing Brian? And what had she been doing in my garden?

Now, I was in a better mindset to ask questions, so as I walked back down the Main Street, I peeked into the clinic. A silhouette walked by the windows as I approached.

I creaked the door open, peering in. If Adanna was with a patient, I shouldn't interrupt. I'd feel guilty monopolizing her time, if she was busy.

She popped her head around a corner. She must have some sort of sixth sense about the door opening. "Skye? Come on in! Are you feeling well?"

I shut the door behind me. "I'm feeling fine, if a bit tired. I don't think I've fully recovered from the jet lag yet. I only arrived in Ireland four days ago."

The doctor frowned. "Most travelers recover in a few days. Are you getting good sleep?"

With a shrug, I said. "Mostly. Better than I usually did in Miami, at any rate. But I didn't come about me."

She sat at her desk and gestured toward one of the chairs facing it. "Sure, and how can I help you today?"

I entwined my fingers to keep them from fidgeting. "I was just trying to find out more about Brian."

Adanna raised her eyebrows but said nothing.

"The guy from my shed, remember?"

She opened her hands, still silent.

Fine. I guess I have to ask. "I was chatting with Seán, and he said that Brian had come into the clinic on Wednesday?"

She didn't hesitate, which reassured me somewhat. "Ah, sure. He came by with an aching head. Normally, I'm not open that late, but I'd been finishing up some reports. I gave him some Paracetamol and sent him on his way. He was a wee bit the worse for drink, as I recall."

"And he didn't have anyone with him?"

Now, she cocked her head. "Him? No, sure and he was alone. Who would he have with him, then? Oh, your dark-haired girl, right?"

"Yes, Cherie. And the other man she was with, Gerald. You didn't see them at all?"

Adanna shook her head with a genuinely puzzled expression just as the door opened behind me.

Gard McCarthy walked in and scowled at me. "Miss O'Shea. What a grand surprise."

I glanced at Adanna as she rose and went to her husband. "Dónal, are you done over at the Flahertys'? Is Patrick feeling better, then?"

He gave her an absent nod but kept his eyes on my face. "I hear you've been asking questions around town, Miss O'Shea. I shouldn't be surprised."

Holding my chin up, I said, "I didn't realize that talking was against the law around here. I've been chatting with a few people, yes."

"It is if you're sticking your nose into my investigation. You're very much like your grandmother, you know."

That made me smile. "Why, thank you."

He growled. "I didn't mean it as a compliment. You've been asking after the dead man."

It was a statement of fact, not a question. Therefore, I didn't feel the need to answer him. Besides, I had been doing exactly that, so I had no real defense.

Adanna tried to guide him out. "I was just discussing a medical issue with Skye. You'll have to interrogate her later."

He refused to leave, still staring at me. "You need to keep out of this matter, Miss O'Shea. Do you understand me?"

I tried to keep my mouth shut. Really, I did. Mostly. However, I had just about had enough of his heavy-handedness. "Only if you're doing your job right. Have you looked into the people who were with him? Cherie and Gerald?"

Gard McCarthy narrowed his eyes. However, to his credit, he pulled out a notebook and let out a long-suffering sigh. "Fine. If it will keep you out of this, I'll write down what you know. Cherie, her name is? What does she look like?"

Here was my chance, but I hesitated. What if he was just looking for proof of my interference with his investigation? I didn't want to end up in trouble. Or worse, deported back to America. I shuddered at that notion. I was already in trouble there for a suspicious death. This would be two. Someone would be bound to notice.

But I needed to see this through. I owed it to myself and my conscience, as well as to Brian, oddly enough. He may have been a jerk, but I found his body, so I was responsible for him, somehow. And to Gran. This was her village, and I needed to make things right.

I gave the Gard details of both Cherie and Gerald, including the fact that she'd been seen arguing on the beach and with Brian at various times of the day before. When I finished, he closed the notebook. "Right. You've passed on your information. That's the end of it. Don't mess in this affair again, or I'll have to take other measures."

He gave me a final glare before he left.

I turned to Adanna. "Will he investigate? Or did he just do that to shut me up?"

She gave me a shrug. "It depends on what mood is upon him. He's usually pretty conscientious about his duty, even if he doesn't like it. He's a good man, Skye, despite occasionally getting into a petty streak. Really, he is."

She sounded like she was trying to convince herself more than me. I had years of experience at that, with Armand, and knew it was useless to try to convince her otherwise. It would only make her dig her heels in to defend him.

After a few pleasantries, I left as my head swam with conflicting emotions. Then I realized that I had forgotten to mention the business card and bent stick of metal. Darn it! If I ran after him now, it would look weird, if not suspicious.

The last thing I needed was him to get twitchy and arrest me under suspicion of murder. Which could lead to a trial. Even if I wasn't convicted, they could easily deport me. Then I'd be without a home, without a life, and without hope.

But I was supposed to be more proactive, right? And if he wasn't going to bother to investigate actual, real clues, then I would. I owed it to Gran to do the right thing, no matter what happened to me. Even if McCarthy ended up shipping me back to Miami.

Once I returned to my house, I grabbed a plastic baggie and went around the back of the Dead Shed. The card and the metal scrap were still there. First, I took another photo with my phone, just to show it in situ. Then, I turned the baggie inside out and carefully picked them both up. Then I pulled the plastic over them and sealed both inside together. If Gard McCarthy decided he *did* want them after all, they wouldn't have my fingerprints all over them. That would be all I needed—another reason for him to suspect me.

I put the plastic baggie in my purse, and then stared at it, sitting on my kitchen counter. My mind was churning with ideas and worries, and I needed to clear it. This was my third day here, and I'd yet to even go down to the beach. Maybe a peaceful walk would help.

As I left the house, instead of turning left to the town center, I turned right. Three streets down, I found a parking lot big enough for about ten cars. Huge, in comparison to other places in this town, but I supposed any beach was a big tourist draw.

Above me, an enormous metal sign rose, looking like someone had attached two Ws together. Then I remembered this was part of the Wild Atlantic Way, a tourist route. A drystone seawall separated the lot from the sand, with a wooden walkway leading down.

A chilly wind shot through me, and I hugged myself, pulling my cardigan tighter. It might be mid-May, but summer had definitely not arrived yet in Ireland. Still, the shore was a fabulous place to think of nothing, so I strolled along the waterline. Gentle waves lapped along the shore, a steady rhythm calming my soul.

Growing up in Miami, I used to visit the beach whenever I could. Of course, the crowds on Miami beaches were usually too much for any sane person to handle, especially during the tourist season, which was September through May. Here, on the shoulder of the summer season, no one else was around. I had the place to myself, and it was glorious.

I stooped to take off my sneakers, and squelched my toes in the cool sand, just damp from the last wave. Soft yellow sand, not the harsh bits of broken shell and rock some beaches had.

The peace of this walk was exactly what I needed. No sounds but the waves lapping on the sand and a few gulls. No people to interrupt my thoughts. No distractions, no phone, no demands upon my attention.

Something blue glinted in the rocks ahead, and I changed my direction so I could examine it. As I turned around the outcrop, I found a statue of the Virgin Mary, face lifted to the sky, her bright blue robes like a beacon. She was nestled into a rocky grotto, with a few offerings left at her feet. Her horde included three tea lights, a length of ribbon, and a heartbreaking pair of baby shoes.

I was no Catholic, but the sight moved me almost to tears. I gave her a respectful nod and moved on, my peace not shattered, but shifted toward melancholy. Who had lost their baby? For what else could the shoes mean?

Finally, I was able to shed my racing speculation and once again surrender to lovely thoughts of nothing.

After about a half mile, a colder wind buffeted me, and I glanced up at the sky. Sure enough, dark clouds were rapidly approaching from the sea. I should turn around. I didn't know the area well enough yet to emerge from a different access lot and know how to get back home.

Just as I turned, though, a flash of color caught my eye. Something very bright pink was flapping in the breeze on the seawall rocks. It almost blew away as I approached, but I caught it. A scarf, a bit battered and torn, but definitely a scarf. Why did that shade of pink seem familiar? I wasn't sure, so I stuck it in my purse until I could remember. It was too torn for the owner to want it back, but I hated to leave litter.

Hurrying back down the sand, the wind whipped my hair and scoured sand on my skin. The first heavy drops pelted down as I climbed the wooden walkway over the seawall to the parking lot.

After shaking the sand off my feet, I shoved my sneakers back on. I didn't want to run on the road in bare feet, despite how nice it had felt walking on the sand. Grit irritated my feet as I jogged the blocks to my house, but I got soaked quickly, and slowed to a walk. I was already drenched. No need to be out of breath, too.

Finally, I got inside and shut the door. I wanted to sink into the comfortable chair, but I needed to get out of these clothes. A hot shower would be blissful.

I pulled myself up the stairs, turned on the shower timer, and peeled off my soaking clothes. When the hot water hit my skin, I gasped. It was both wonderful and too hot at the same time.

When I finished, I reluctantly left the delightful heat and got dressed again. Then I finally glanced at the clock. It was already five? Where had the day gone? Had I slipped into some fairy world and lost time?

I opened a can of beef stew, poured it into a bowl, and stuck it in the microwave. Should I have coffee, too? I was still shivering, despite the hot shower. No, it was too late for coffee. I'd have too much trouble sleeping. Maybe tea, then?

The microwave beeped, and I pulled out the steaming bowl, grabbed a spoon, and sat at the counter.

Ah, delightful soup. A perfect remedy for the chills. Especially the running-in-the-cold-rain chills.

Something hit my legs, and I glanced down. Faelan was glaring up at me. "Oh? And what do you want? I fed you this morning, so don't give me that look."

"Mrow!"

"Not talking yet, are you? I wish I understood the rules. When can you talk, and when can't you? Or was I dreaming that time?"

"Mrow!"

I rolled my eyes. "Fine. Whatever. Go do your cat things."

Maybe I wasn't cut out to be a cat owner. I had no idea what he wanted.

Once I finished my stew, I made a cup of chamomile tea and retired to the comfy chair. Faelan jumped into my lap almost immediately, and began his motorboat purring.

"Is that what you wanted? A soft lap? Well, I can give you that." I petted him a few times. Between his purring and his soft fur, my stress and troubles melted away. Having a cat might be worth something, after all.

"I wish you would talk again. I'd ask you about Cherie and Gerald. And Brian."

Faelan's purring halted abruptly, and I glanced at the cat. He was staring right at me. Without breaking our locked gazes, he walked to the diary and stood on it. Then he proceeded to groom his paws, as if he didn't have a care in the world.

"Right. Message received loud and clear, commander."

I pulled the diary out from under Faelan and started reading again. I had no idea what, in particular, I was looking for, but I recognized a mandate when I saw it.

CHAPTER TWELVE

I woke the next morning and couldn't move my neck. That wasn't surprising, as I had fallen asleep reading Gran's diary.

With great care, I put the book on the side table and pushed myself to my feet. Every muscle in my body protested as I creaked and groaned.

The soft, misty day didn't help, especially as the temperature had dropped. Gray clouds and drizzle made everything muted and dim. What a great first Saturday in Ireland. The sun might have been somewhere out there, trying to burn through it all, but failing horribly.

Once I showered and dressed, I had a relaxing morning with my coffee and read a bit more in Gran's diary. This section was about the O'Shea family crypt. This entry was only about five years ago.

Dear Diary:

I went to visit Seán today. I do that every year on our anniversary, with a bit of chocolate. He did love his sweets, like. I promised to leave a Flake bar for him each year. He said it would be better than any stupid candle in the chapel.

Well, just as I was leaving, an eerie howl surrounded me. It was a soft, misty day, and the sound was distorted. I was a bit worried about some animal being hurt. Sure, and some would say it was the Dearg-Due or a Bean Sídhe, but who did I have who could die? No one nearby, at any rate.

Instead, something rustled in the bushes behind the crypt. Normally, I have the place to myself, so I went in search of whatever was making such a ruckus. And what do you think I saw? A huge black cat! He slammed against my legs, and I swear he nearly knocked me on my arse. Big, heavy thing, he was.

I gave him a thorough pet and then went to leave, but he followed me. What could I do but let him inside? So now, Faelan lives with us.

So, Faelan was a stray that adopted Gran. I flashed a smile at the shadows, where Faelan was curled up next to the radiator.

I was about to keep reading when someone knocked on my door. After a quick glance at myself to ensure I wasn't a total mess, I went to the pub door. This seemed to be the generally accepted front door, even if the house front door was on the other side.

Bright blue eyes and a sunny grin greeted me. "Good morning, Skye!"

My heartbeat sped up a little. "Seán! How nice to see you. Won't you come in for some tea?" *Yay, more tea.* My body would be more tea than water within a month.

He flashed a grin. "That's kind of you, Skye. Coffee would hit better, if you have any?"

I chuckled, guiding him into the parlour. He settled on the settee as I poured a cup from my carafe. "Do you take milk or sugar?"

I was getting to be an old hand at this *if someone visits, you must offer them a drink* thing. It was like all I did now is drink with a visitor, or drink as a visitor at someone else's place.

We sat for a moment in silence, sipping our drinks, before Seán launched out with, "I was hoping you weren't thinking me too rude yesterday."

I furrowed my brow. "Rude? Whatever for?"

He stared into his cup. "I sort of blew off some of your questions, and I wanted to apologize. I have no real reason to be evasive."

I still had no idea what he meant.

My visitor let out a deep breath. A flash of something crossed his face, and while it could have been my imagination, it seemed like he paled. Hard to tell, as there wasn't a huge amount of natural light, though. Then he shrugged. "I didn't want to mention that I'd seen Brian that night at O'Leary's."

Sudden suspicion swept over me. Normally, people didn't lie unless there was a reason. It might not be a good reason, but they'd still have a reason. "Why didn't you want to say anything?"

He rubbed the back of his neck. "Well, we sort of got into a bit of a discussion. And I didn't want to seem like the same sort of angry man he was."

With a rueful chuckle, I waved my hand. "Don't worry. I don't see you as the same sort at all. It sounds like you knew him. I thought he was a visitor here?"

My guest gave a shrug. "I'd met him a few times, but we weren't best mates or anything."

"Do you know his last name?"

Sean shook his head as he took another sip of coffee. "Not even that. We barely exchanged a few dozen words, truth be told."

My courage must have returned due to being on my turf. I wasn't about to let this chance go. "Angry words, were they?"

He didn't answer at first, then he gave a sheepish grin. "I suppose so. I was upset at him for the accident, you see."

"*My* accident?"

Rubbing the back of his neck, he nodded. "Aye, yours. I was telling him he needed to either be more careful or to leave town, because ours was a peaceful town. No place for the likes of him."

It was my turn to feel sheepish. Here, I'd been assuming the worst about someone who had come to my rescue. Twice, even.

But Seán still wouldn't meet my gaze, so I guessed there was something else he wasn't saying. "And when you finished with him, what happened?"

He ducked his head. "Ah, well, I shouldn't like to say."

Raising my eyebrows, I took a sip of coffee. It was growing cold. "Shouldn't you?"

Sean stayed silent for several moments, but I kept my eyes on him, channeling my nurse authority. Finally, he let out a sigh. "I wanted to stay, to make sure he behaved, but I went out drinking in Schull with some mates."

"So, you don't know what he got up to afterward?"

"No, that's the last time I saw him. The next morning, the town was abuzz with the news of his death and you discovering him in your shed."

Another rush of unease swept over me, and I wanted to avoid talking about that particular incident, so I changed the subject. "I appreciate you being honest with me. Really, I do. Now, I have a totally unrelated question for you. Adanna mentioned that you were handy with repairs, is that correct?"

Sean blinked a few times. "Sure, and I am, but only with the little things. Some basic carpentry, electrics, and the like. If you have some larger project, I'd call on the cousins."

That was an odd name for a company? "Is that a local construction business?"

He chuckled and shook his head. "Ah, no, that's Finn and Rory Lynch. They do odd jobs for most of us. They're good enough, but they need strong supervision. Don't just tell them what to do and leave them to it, right?"

We exchanged grins. "Message received loud and clear. I made a list of things to fix. Could you take a look to see if you can do any of them?" I went to the kitchen to fetch my pad and handed it to him. I hastily added, "I'd pay for your time, of course."

He traced his finger down the items. "Lights, sure, I can replace those. Cracked window, cracked stool. I don't know anything about the taps, but Cormac might help you with those. And for the supplier names, though he might be cagey about some contacts." He glanced up. "Don't trust that one as far as you can throw him. He does a lot for the community, but only when it's to his benefit."

The corner of my mouth turned up. "I'd figured out that one on my own."

"Grand. Let's see, what else do you have here? New bulb for the hallway, door handle. Sure, I can help you with most of these. Even the garden, if you want some help there. I'd check in with Joshua and Indira for that."

"Joshua? Is he the guy who runs the café?"

Sean nodded as he handed me the list back. "Sure, he and his wife, Indira. They're full of ideas for self-sufficiency and living off the land and would love to help you get there yourself. You'd just have to listen to them nattering on about climate change and all that."

"He seemed like a nice enough guy. Where do they live?"

"Over near the churchyard, just past the cemetery."

That reminded me of the crypt. My eyes flicked to Gran's diary, which was still sitting on the table next to my chair. Maybe

I should ask Seán about some of the things she wrote about. I turned to pick it up.

Faelan chose that moment to leap out of nowhere into my lap, startling me out of three years of growth. "Yikes!"

This, of course, caused me to spill my now-cold coffee all over the cat, my lap, and the comfy chair. A few drops even made it to the rug. Faelan launched from my lap, gouging through my jeans, and even drawing blood on my thigh.

Sean jumped up and ran for the kitchen and came back with a roll of paper towels. He mopped up the chair and rug but stopped at patting down my jeans. I gave him a wry smile. "Thanks, but I think I can get the rest."

The scratches stung, but I was more peeved with my jeans being ripped. However, I didn't want to show my temper to my visitor. Even if I wasn't interested in him, that wouldn't be neighborly.

"Are you sure you're fine?"

"Yeah, I'm alright. I need to go change and dab some antibiotic on these."

He glanced toward the door. "I should be going, anyhow. Maybe I can come back tomorrow afternoon and start working on those repairs for you?"

With a grateful smile, I said, "That would be grand."

Sean laughed. "See, you're getting the lingo already."

Once my visitor left, I stomped upstairs, gingerly removed my jeans, and searched the cabinet for some sort of Neosporin or something. I found some Mercurochrome. Really? That was ancient. Wasn't it toxic or something?

I shrugged. It shouldn't be too dangerous to use just one time. I'd add Neosporin to my next shopping trip. I needed to clean these cuts, since I had no idea what Faelan got into outside.

Once I cleaned the wounds and slapped some band-aids on them, I put on an intact pair of jeans and went back downstairs. I peered around for the betraying feline. "Alright, Cat! Come out. I know you're there somewhere."

A shadow twitched. That must be him in the corner. "You have some explaining to do. What was all that with my lap?"

Faelan sauntered out with his nose and tail in the air, as if he hadn't just torn my thigh to ribbons. Then he walked around my legs and between them, purring like a normal cat.

"Right." I snatched him up and sat in the comfy chair, and held him by the scruff of the neck, so he had to look into my eyes. *Oof, he's heavier than I thought.* "What's the big idea, huh? Do you have some objection to Seán?"

He tried to move his head, but couldn't with me holding him. I pursed my lips and put him gently back on my lap. "I swear to all that's holy, Faelan. If you scratch me again..."

With deliberate movements, he stood on the diary. Then he sat and started grooming his face.

"The diary? You didn't want me to show Seán the diary?"

The huge black cat nodded once, then went back to grooming.

"Fine. I won't show it to him. Is there anyone else on your hit list?"

The cat cocked his head and I swear he smiled. Then he growled.

"I wish you were in one of your talking moods. This charades thing is ridiculous. There *is* someone else? Or maybe you don't want me to show anyone Gran's diary?"

Faelan let out a huge yowl, nodded his head, and jumped to the floor. In an instant, he had disappeared back into the shadows.

Shaking my head at his strange ways, I grabbed the diary and picked up where I'd left off, reading about the family crypt.

Faelan fit right into the house, without any trouble. He's a sassy one, I'll give him that. It took him several months to warm up to me, though I'm sure he appreciated the food and shelter. But he helps me out with some advice now and then.

I stared at that paragraph. Faelan helped Gran out with advice. So, I wasn't dreaming, after all? That made me feel a bit better. Armand had always waved away things I saw or heard. When I mentioned people's colors, or the strange music haunting my mind, he said I must be going nuts. I almost believed him.

This time, however, I had proof of someone else hearing Faelan talk. At least, that's what it looked like from her description.

Faelan has been a great help with so many things. He even helped me figure out why I was seeing colors on people.

Colors on people? That sounded like me. The reds, yellows, blues. From what I could tell from stories and asking others, no one else could do this. But I'd seen them since I was a child. I stopped asking about it, as I'd always gotten strange looks, but evidently Gran had it, too.

I scanned the next few paragraphs, but she went on about a neighbor's wake. I wish she'd written more about the colors. Of course, as magical powers go, that wasn't exactly a powerful legacy. Couldn't I have gotten something more useful, like turning invisible or being able to teleport?

I kept reading, but the next few pages were still about the wake, the funeral, and then the burial of her neighbor.

Idly, I wondered what our family crypt looked like. Would Gran be buried there? She must be. I hadn't even thought of asking the solicitor. I would like to see where my grandfather was buried. Would it be a fancy building, or something simple and sober?

Suddenly taken with the notion that I had to see it, I closed the diary and, in case someone else should visit who Faelan objected to, piled a few other random books on top of it. Then, I practically ran out of the house. I glanced up at the church spire and made a beeline for it, half walking, half running. I just passed the art gallery on the corner and turned right when someone called my name.

"Skye?"

I turned to see Adanna across the street and gave her a wave. "Hey! Are you off for a house call?"

She shook her head. "Just finished one, but it was quicker than I'd planned. Would you like to share a cuppa? Where are you going?"

I glanced back toward my house, and almost said yes. A cup of tea in my cozy front room would be lovely. But I'd had enough tea and coffee with guests for a while. That's all I'd done since I got here.

Almost as if she stood behind me, I heard Gran's words. *A guest should always be offered tea, and it would be rude to refuse it when visiting.* If I did any more visiting, I would slosh with every step.

I made my voice all spooky. "I'm headed to the graveyard. OooOOoohhh!"

Adanna let out a huge laugh. "Sure and it's a lovely stroll. I'll come with you."

We walked around the church to the extensive graveyard behind it. Trees shaded the hilly area, in some areas so thick you could barely see through in the middle of the day. "This must be very atmospheric at night."

The doctor said, "Even more so in the fog. A proper haunted place, it is, too."

I couldn't tell if she believed that or not. She had, after all, told me stories of the Fair Folk the other day, as if they were real. Of course, some were real, like my cat. But Adanna wouldn't know that. Or would she?

I stood at the elaborate iron gate entrance, scanning the soft green hills, enormous trees, and shrub barriers.

"Do you know where my family crypt is?"

"It's just over there." Adanna pointed to the right, along the stone wall. Tall bushes surrounded a square building made of stone. The shadows painted it a deep blue, and a willow tree arched overhead, long branches sweeping the ground on the other side.

Silently, I approached, noting the details. A waist-high iron fence surrounded it, rusty in spots, painted black in others. It needed some maintenance. The green double doors had Celtic knotwork, as did the pointed arch doorway. Four Roman pillars decorated the front, and two more in the back corners, from where I could see.

"Gran is buried here? And my grandfather, too?"

"Aye, she'd accept no other place, to be sure."

"Did… did she have a funeral?"

Adanna waved her hand. "Oh, sure, most of the village came to pay their respects. We had a grand wake at McCarthy's, too."

I ran my hand across the Celtic knotwork on the door, then tried the door, but it was locked. I glanced back at Adanna with raised eyebrows.

"Father Fraser will have the keys. He keeps them all for folks who want to visit their ancestors."

I stared at the door again. "My ancestors. I never felt that I had family, being isolated in Miami. Are there any other members of the family living close by? Cousins? Aunts? Uncles?"

Adanna frowned for a moment, then shook her head, her eyes downcast. "No, I don't think so. A few distant cousins out in the hills, perhaps. None close enough to your grandmother to come to her funeral. And for an Irishman, that's saying something."

We shared a rueful chuckle at that.

"What happened to them all?"

The doctor shrugged as she glanced around the graveyard. "They all just sort of… moved away. Your grandmother was the last of your line in this part of the world. The final holder of her legacy. At least," and now she gave me a big grin, "until you came along!"

A chill ran down my spine at her words, though I had no idea why.

Despite my earlier insistence on no more coffee or tea, I needed something warm inside of me. "I think I could use that cuppa now. But not at my house. I want to be out and about. Do you like the Blarney Scone?"

She gave a nod, and we headed back toward the gate. "Sure, the Fields have a lovely shop. Have you met them, yet?"

I carefully stepped over a root. "I've met Joshua. He seems nice enough. Though Seán warned me he might proselytize a bit on climate change."

Adanna rolled her eyes as she closed the graveyard gate behind us. Then, she latched it firmly and tested it before turning away. "He's one to talk, with his bees and all."

"Why do you latch it? Couldn't someone just unlatch it to get in?"

She stared at me for a moment. "Graveyard walls aren't there to keep people *out*, Skye."

Adanna and I shared a quiet cup of vegetable soup at the Blarney Scone. Joshua's place was busier today, but that made sense for a Saturday. The café wasn't nearly as quiet, but it still felt homey and comforting.

Afterward, I waved goodbye to Adanna as she went back to her clinic, and I sauntered back home. I wasn't sure what I was searching for at the crypt, but I was glad to have seen it. There was something anchoring about visiting a place where generations of your family were at rest. A sense of permanence. A sense of belonging.

A sense that I'd never felt before, except for brief glimpses at Gran's house when I was a child.

Slowly, carefully, I was gathering those glimpses together and knitting together my new life. A few bits were broken or shattered, but I was beginning to gain confidence I could have the time and support to mend them. Or maybe replace a few of the broken ones.

With these rosy thoughts twinkling in my mind, I opened the door to the pub.

Something crunched under my shoe. Crunch? What would crunch? I turned on the light, but remembered the electrics weren't on in the pub yet. I flicked on my phone flashlight. Broken glass?

I glanced over at the boarded windows, but they were all intact except the one which had already been broken. Then I peered into the house and gasped.

Everything was a mess. Drawers were pulled out. Things were strewn everywhere. Broken glasses littered the kitchen floor. Glancing back toward the pub, I realized someone must have broken some of the bottles from the wall.

Someone had broken in. Chills ran down my spine and suddenly, I wanted a gun. I used to carry one in Miami. It only made sense when I came home from night shifts. Here, I couldn't have one.

My next thought was to call the police. But Gard McCarthy's crappy attitude kept me from that notion.

I scanned the kitchen counter and let out a sigh of relief that my purse was still there. I rifled through it and found my wallet and my keys.

But no baggie.

I looked again, taking everything out carefully. Definitely no sign of the plastic baggie or its contents.

But who would know I even had that? Unless someone watched me when I picked them up.

Despite it being summer and midday, everything turned cold.

Something crashed out back, and every muscle in my body screamed at me to run away. Then, I remembered my determination to be braver.

So, instead of hiding or fleeing, I grabbed the first thing I could find that might work as a weapon–the iron fire poker–and peered out the back window into the garden.

The metal weight felt good in my hand. *It will be a worthy weapon*. I chanted that under my breath as I glanced to the left and right, trying to figure out if anyone was out there. Nothing moved.

Was I being brave or was I being stupid? Probably a bit of both. I was okay with that.

With a clammy hand, I opened the back door. Of course, it creaked loud enough to wake the dead.

The wind chose that moment to pick up and rustle every leaf in my yard, as well as some fabric fluttering in the wind somewhere. A flag? Someone's laundry? I had no idea.

Step by step, I crept to the first shed. The door was slightly ajar. Had I left it open? I couldn't remember. With my heart in my throat, I pushed the door open with the poker, then held it out with both hands, ready to swing at whatever leapt out at me.

Nothing did.

I took a ragged breath and tiptoed to the second shed. The Dead Shed. This door was firmly shut. Praying to whatever gods might be listening that I didn't find a second body inside, I poked it open, my entire body tensed.

Dark silence greeted me.

Despite my better judgment and my screaming nerves, I turned my phone flashlight on and examined each shadowy corner, hoping to find precisely nothing.

CHAPTER THIRTEEN

Once I was back inside, I managed to make a cup of chamomile tea without my hands shaking too much. Mostly.

I had no idea what to do. Calling the Gard seemed like a lesson in futility, since he obviously had a chip on his shoulder about me. Still, I didn't want to be in this house alone.

Despite my worries, I looked up the website, found the number, and dialed it, but got a busy signal.

A busy signal? Had I traveled back in time to the twentieth century? How could a Gard station have only one line? I hung up with disgust.

Was someone *trying* to frighten me? If so, they were doing a darn good job! Armand used to do that. He thought it was hilarious to jumpscare at me, then laugh when I was honestly frightened.

I wouldn't miss that part of my old life at all.

But someone was trying to rattle me. Maybe to make me leave? Who would want to do that? McCarthy was a snotrag, but I didn't think he would stoop to this. He seemed much too straight-laced and professional for that.

The other pub owner? He seemed the slightly slimy type. Seán did warn me that he wasn't above underhanded tactics to get what he wanted. As the owner of the only other pub in town, he had true, financial reasons to run me off.

As each of these realizations drilled into my brain, I sunk further and further down in the comfy chair, pulling my legs up until I was a curled-up miserable ball of worry.

Faelan yowled and jumped onto the settee. He stared at me.

"What?"

He just cocked his head and stared some more.

"Leave me alone. I want to be miserable for a while," I said.

The cat didn't leave, but he did stop staring at me, at least. I snaked my arm out and got my cup. I wrapped my hands around it, drawing comfort from the heat.

Each sip of tea warmed my body, but not my nerves. I made the mistake of looking around and saw the mess from the break-in still surrounding me, consuming me, piling upon me. Stress and fright made my hackles rise, as if I was as much a cat as Faelan. I needed to unkink my muscles.

I'd never been a huge practitioner of yoga, but a friend in college had taught me the basics. Maybe they'd help now.

First, I scrolled through my phone to put on some soothing music. I smiled when I saw Enya. Not only perfectly soothing, but apropos to Ireland.

Then, I moved the coffee table to one side, so I had space on the rug. I stood. facing the fireplace. Then I closed my eyes and just breathed.

In through my nose, out through my mouth. In and out. In and out. I became aware of every muscle used in breathing. In and out. Then, I lifted my hands into the Mountain pose, as if I was ready to dive off a board.

I held that for a while, then stepped back with one foot, into a lunge position. Up again into Mountain, then back with the other foot.

Faelan padded to a spot underneath me in the lunge, his tail tickling my chin. "C'mon, cat. Go away," I rumbled.

"Rowl."

"You heard me. I'm trying to get zen here. You aren't helping."

After about twenty minutes or so, my anxiety eased. My tea was cold, but I didn't want more, anyhow. I glanced at the clock; it was only four. A bit too early for dinner, unless I was a senior citizen hunting an early bird special.

I didn't want to go for a walk. The idea that someone had been watching me made me want to curl up again.

But no. I wouldn't curl up. I wouldn't be frightened. Wasn't I supposed to be taking charge of my life? Being in charge of my life meant not letting some jumped-up, power-hungry jerk run me out of town.

Not gonna happen.

And I didn't care if Gard McCarthy dismissed my report. There was a break-in. There was evidence. I wanted it on record in case the harassment continued.

I just couldn't mention the baggie with the business card or the metal fragment.

My determination came back with a vengeance. Almost grabbing my purse to head to the Gard station, I realized it was evidence. I should leave it in place. But what if the burglar came back? I slung the strap on my shoulder.

Gingerly picking my way back through the pub, I left and locked the door. Then I stopped.

The door *had* been locked. So had the back door. All of the windows were still locked, too. Whoever had broken into my house had a key.

Unless they could make themselves as small as Faelan and go through his door.

Now serious chills cascaded through my veins. What if my burglar wasn't… human?

Visions of Banshees and Dearg-Due swirled in my mind, until I literally shook my head to dispel them. No, I was being silly. Of course, the burglar was human. Someone had my key. Or rather, Gran's key. That might be anyone. I had no idea who she might have trusted with it, other than Adanna.

The walk to the Gard station blurred by as my mind still whirled with ideas, worries, and possibilities. By the time I reached the door, I had to take a deep breath and calm myself before I turned the knob.

Inside, I glanced around. Pristine white walls bore very little in way of decoration. Some posters and notices. Phone numbers for emergencies both here and in Schull. A counter with no one behind it.

I stepped further in, listening for anyone. The door hadn't been locked, as it had before, so someone should be here. "Hello?"

McCarthy's voice called out, "Just a moment!"

Then, a toilet flushed, and I suppressed a smile. Somehow, imagining McCarthy with his pants around his ankles made him less worrisome. Or at least, a bit comical.

McCarthy came out of a back hallway, and his expression turned sour when he saw me. "Yes? What now?"

"Is that any way to greet a neighbor?" *Strains of Mister Roger's Neighborhood* ran through my mind.

"You're not a neighbor," he growled, "you're a foreigner pushing their way into our town. And an O'Shea, to boot."

That took me aback. I didn't realize he felt so… well… insular? Xenophobic? Whatever the right word was. A lout, either way.

"I need to report a burglary."

His eyebrows rose. "Do you, now? Where is this, then?"

I rolled my eyes with an exasperated sigh. "Where do you think it is? At my house and the pub. There were broken bottles in the pub, someone went through all my things in the parlour, broke dishes in the kitchen."

McCarthy pursed his lips as he grabbed a notepad and started writing. "Was anything missing?"

Only a baggie I can't tell you about. "Not that I could see, but I'm still not sure of all the things my grandmother had, so I might not be able to tell."

He wrote without looking up at me, and asked in a bored voice, "How did they get in?"

"I'm not sure. I didn't notice any windows broken, and both doors were locked."

The Gard glanced up at that. "Oh, really? That's fascinating. Does anyone else have a key to your place?"

The corner of my mouth quirked up. "I understand you have a set."

The scowl on his face could have made milk curdle at twenty paces. "You can be assured, Miss O'Shea, I did *not* burgle your home. Who else?" He bent over his pad again.

I gave a shrug. "I'm not sure. Gran might have given keys to everyone in town, for all I know. Changing the locks is on my to-do list."

He put down the pen and glared at me. "You aren't taking this very seriously, Miss O'Shea. One would think you aren't telling me the entire truth."

Well, he was absolutely correct. I wasn't telling the entire truth, and I couldn't. If I described the missing baggie and its contents, the Gard would either arrest me for interfering again, or question my sanity.

And I wasn't taking this very seriously. Images of him squatting over the toilet kept popping up in my mind. It was better than the frightening idea of someone watching me invading, so I welcomed it.

"Does this have anything to do with the homicide?"

My eyes widened as my heart beat faster. "Oh, it's a homicide, then? Not a natural death?"

Crossing his arms, he said, "That's not yet determined. But yes, we're treating it as a homicide. Now, that's not knowledge to go blabbing around the pub, mind you."

I clenched my teeth. "I'm no gossip."

"That's as may be, but it sounds like you enjoy being the center of attention. First the murder, now a burglary. Anything to be in the spotlight, eh?"

The Gard emphasized his point with a scowl that looked straight out of a cartoon. I almost managed to stifle my giggle but didn't quite succeed.

That made it worse. His scowl deepened, if that was even possible. Then, he walked around the desk and grabbed my arm. "Right, then. Miss O'Shea, I am going to detain you on suspicion of wasting police time."

I pulled back. "What? You can't be serious. I'm reporting a break-in! Aren't you even going to go look?"

Evidently, McCarthy didn't take kindly to being mocked. "I am quite serious. Come with me."

Gard McCarthy yanked on my arm. I tried to jerk out of his grip, but he was surprisingly strong for such a lanky man. Flashes of memories from Armand hammered me, and I struggled to breathe. "Wait! No, you can't just chuck me in a cell. Whatever happened to due process?"

Gard McCarthy pulled me relentlessly into the room behind the desk and toward a hallway, and my mind screamed to get away. Being held prisoner by a man was something I could never tolerate again. I struggled and pulled, and for a moment, I slipped from his grip, but I didn't get far. He just caught me again, grasping my arm so tight, I whimpered in pain.

"I can do what I like, Miss O'Shea. All I have to do is call the Immigration Service and report you, and they'll boot you out of Ireland faster than you can say, *help, help, I'm being repressed!*"

Obviously, he wasn't going to be budged. Maybe someone close by could hear me. As loud as I could, I shouted, "Adanna! Adanna, help!"

"None of that! She's out on a call, anyhow."

Quicker than I would have thought, he'd shoved me into one of three cells and locked the door. These cells didn't have bars, like in the movies, but proper rooms with one little window about one foot wide and tall. Even if I was as skinny as a child, I wouldn't make it through that.

Everything was off-white, pristinely clean, and… empty. The only feature in the room was a platform of a sort along one wall, solidly built and painted a sickly yellow, which could be either a chair or a bed. Folded blankets and a pillow were piled on one end.

There was a raised metal circle in the other corner. I could guess what that was for.

I sat down and closed my eyes, trying to find peace. Trying to soothe my racing heart and my frantic brain. My brain was sometimes a dope, and lately, it had been a real stinker.

Breathe in, breathe out. Like with yoga; in and out. In and out.

Slowly, my panic trickled away, and I was able to think again in a mostly rational manner.

What did he actually have me on? He had no proof that I was wasting police time, because he hadn't gone to investigate. He did keep mentioning my last name. Perhaps he had some sort of mafia-style vendetta against Gran? Or someone else in the family.

But instead of giving me the benefit of the doubt, he just assumed I was some attention-seeking drama queen.

No, I'd never wanted attention or drama. I wanted contentment. I wanted safety. I wanted peace and warmth and comfort.

At least this cell was peaceful. I supposed it was safe, too. At least until Gard McCarthy called Immigration.

Having grown up in Miami, I had a rather jaded opinion of immigration services. So many people escaped Cuba over the years, fleeing oppression and threats of death, only to be deported the moment they reached freedom.

Fermented sheep nuggets. I had the right to be here in Ireland. I'd fought for months through my lawyers to obtain the proper visas. As soon as it went through, I would be able to claim citizenship, since my mother was born in Ireland. However, that process took time. My lawyer said up to three years, and it had only been months since I applied.

In the meantime, snotrags like Gard McCarthy could, indeed, threaten me with deportation. If I did do something to break the law, they could boot me out faster than the devil can fly.

Despite my situation, I chuckled to myself, as that was one of Gran's expressions. I'd always found it colorful and used it often.

I took another deep breath and tried to piece together everything that had been going on. There had to be a pattern to things. Some sort of reason for what has happened, right?

Brian came into town a few days before I did, according to Seán. At least by Tuesday, though it could have been earlier.

He'd been seen a few times around town with Cherie, but not her companion. Had they arrived together or separately? Who had the other guy been? Cherie's friend? Another lover? Brian's lover? A sibling? I had no idea.

Someone shouted outside, and I peered out of the window. Just that band of boys in their ragged punk clothing. One of them noticed me and pointed. "Oi! Look at herself! All locked up, like! The Shades caught her!"

The rest laughed. "Throw away the key!" They walked away with great hilarity. My face burned with embarrassment. To be seen in jail by such as them? Then I chided myself for my prejudice. Just because they looked rough didn't make them bad people. Well, looked rough and smacked my car as they walked by.

Back to my puzzle. Where was I? I couldn't even remember. I'd never been great at keeping things in memory. Well, except for medication details. Those, I was trained in. Murder clues? Not so much.

Sean said he saw Cherie and another man arguing on the beach, which must have been when she lost her pink scarf. That was still in my purse, which was out in the Gard office. McCarthy had yanked it off my shoulder when he shoved me in here. So, they must have been on the beach before I arrived, right? I was already losing track of the days and times.

Then I arrived in, as O'Leary put it, a spectacular fashion. Brian hit my car, Cherie argued with him, and then went off with Gerald.

My mind was beginning to spin with all the facts. I wish I had paper to write all this down and keep track of it, but at least it was keeping my mind off being in a literal jail cell.

After that, Seán said Brian and Cherie went to the clinic to get some painkillers, though Adanna only saw Brian. My head was beginning to hurt with the convolutions.

Another sound from outside broke my concentration, and I tried to ignore it. I wanted to growl at whoever it was, *Be quiet!* I was trying to concentrate.

Someone must have broken into Adanna's clinic that same night, since she discovered it the next day. The next morning, I revisited the Dead Shed and found the card and metal stick. I shuddered again with the realization that someone must have been watching me, to know to steal it from me.

When did I go to the beach and find the scarf? I couldn't even remember now. I went to the crypt. Was that the same day? I hadn't even been here a week and the days were melding together. That jet lag must have done a number on me. Of course, keeping track of days was easier when I had to work shifts.

After that, I went home to find it burgled. Then, like a prime dolt, I came here to report the crime. As if McCarthy was going to act like an adult for once.

Why did he hate me so? Was it just because I was an American, pushing my way in, as he said? Or was there something else? My nosiness into this case? My budding friendship with Adanna?

That could be it. Husbands didn't like their wives paying more attention to someone else. Armand had made that painfully clear to me often enough.

Someone was talking outside the window. Frustration bubbled up inside me and I leapt to my feet to tell them to shut up. Then I recognized Adanna's voice. "Adanna! Adanna, I need help in here!"

She stopped talking to Máiréad and turned, her eyes growing wide. "Wait there!"

I rolled my eyes. "Well, what do you think I'm going to do, fly away?" But she was already hurrying to the station front door around the corner.

A heated argument filtered down the hallway. I didn't catch most of it, as they kept their tones low, but I made out a few snippets from the Gard. *What do you think you're pulling?* And *You know she's trouble.*

Trouble. Me? I was never trouble. I was the low-key, low-maintenance woman. That was my brand. Still, I did seem to be getting into a lot of messes here, and I'd only been here a few days. Maybe the Gard wasn't as wrong as I thought.

Gard McCarthy stomped down the hall, unlocked my door, and opened it wide. His expression looked like someone had stolen his favorite gift on Christmas. He mumbled out a growling, "You're free to go, Miss O'Shea."

I kept my chin high as I walked past him. Being petty would only throw oil on the fire. "Thank you."

Adanna was holding my purse. "Here, this must be yours." She shot a glare back at her husband. "And stop harassing her!"

"I'm just doing my job, Adanna! And Miss O'Shea?"

I turned back, my heart skipping a beat in case he changed his mind. "You're free on your own recognizance, but don't let me catch you meddling in my homicide case again. Is that understood?"

Adanna walked with me back home. Which was fantastic, because I was shaken as heck. After my bravado with Gard McCarthy, my courage fled like a frightened rabbit.

As we walked into the pub, Adanna helped me avoid the broken bottles, then into my chair. "What happened in here? Was there a fight?"

I shook my head, still numb. "No, someone broke in. Well, not broke in. They must have had a key. But they broke things and tore things apart. That's what I went to the Gard station to report. Except your husband decided I was some attention-seeker trying to stir up drama." I couldn't keep the bitterness from my voice.

Then my eyes fell upon the side table, where Gran's diary had been. It wasn't there. Neither were the two books that I piled on top of it.

Frantically, I jumped to my feet and began to search for it. How could I have let that get stolen? Gran had entrusted her precious journal to me, and I'd lost it in just a few days.

"Skye? What are you looking for? What's missing?"

Faelan wouldn't want me to tell anyone about the diary. But I didn't care if Faelan didn't approve of Adanna just now. I needed all the help I could get. "Gran's diary. It was on that table. Big leather-bound book, decorated with Celtic knotwork."

"Oh, I've seen that before."

Interesting.

I scanned each of the bookshelves, getting more and more frantic. What if I'd lost it? I would never be able to have that part of Gran, and she'd be gone forever. Then the kitchen, and even in the bar. Finally, Adanna asked, "Is this it?"

I glanced down the hallway to find her carrying an open book. It was the diary, and my heart calmed again. "Yes, that's it. Why are you carrying it like that?"

She came into the parlour and placed it on the coffee table. "It was open like this, in the laundry room. Sort of like someone had been reading it and was interrupted? I thought you'd want to know what page they were on."

Gran's gruesome sketch of the Dearg-Due stared back at me, its fiery eyes staring into my fear.

I looked into Adanna's eyes and then back down to the sketch. Something made my skin crawl and I went to close the book, but Adanna stopped me. "No, wait. I need to tell you about it."

"About what?"

"That." She pointed to the drawing and sat down on the settee. I took the chair again. This was all feeling very odd to me.

Even though I suspected the answer was *no,* I asked, "It's just a tale, right? A myth?"

Instead of answering, the doctor took a deep breath. "The Dearg-Due is a specific type of the Fair Folk. Just like the banshee, it is attached to an event or a family."

"Which family?"

She pressed her lips together. "I shouldn't say much more. This is ancient history."

Faelan chose that moment to jump on her lap, and the doctor startled back. "Oh!"

The cat stared straight into her eyes and placed a paw on her hand. Then he glanced at the diary on the table. Adanna gave him a nod. "I guess I have to."

"Which family, Adanna?"

I didn't want to hear her say it. "Yours."

CHAPTER FOURTEEN

Sitting in my Gran's parlour, the world wobbled beneath me. I just couldn't believe what I was hearing. Adanna was a doctor. A woman of science. She couldn't possibly be saying that there was some fairy creature haunting my family. Could she?

Then again, I was a nurse, and Faelan talked to me. So I'd better stop throwing stones, hadn't I? I drew in a ragged breath, trying not to let panic take over.

"There are several families around here that have some connection with the Fair Folk. Yours, mine, even Cormac's, though he'd never admit it. We all remember the tales, the stories, from our parents and grandparents."

"And what was the story from my grandmother?"

Adanna pointed to the sketch. "That. Her father, his name was Sweeney. He was… well, he wasn't a nice man."

I swallowed and gave her a nod.

"So, this Sweeney, he was known to have an eye for the ladies. And he seduced this woman, the bride of another man.

Her name was Dierdre Brennan, and well named she was. That means sorrow, right?"

I gave another nod as if I knew that, but my mind was racing. I was trying to figure out what this all had to do with some fairy creature.

"So, Dierdre's husband, Gerald Brennan, found out about the affair. He begged Dierdre to return, that he'd take her back, but she wanted to stay with your great-grandfather."

I hoped this would pivot into some lovely romantic story, but I suspected that wasn't going to happen.

"Remember how I said he wasn't a nice man? Well, your grandfather spurned her, very publicly. Literally threw her to the ground in the middle of the street, beside the market cross. After that, Gerald couldn't take her back. She'd been branded as a wanton, and back then, that was damning."

Now, I was perched on the edge of the chair. "Then what?"

Adanna let out a sad sigh. "Then, they found the poor wee girl face down in the river. The husband insisted that Sweeney had killed her. Sweeney insisted that Gerald had, or that she'd taken her own life. Whatever the truth was, she was gone, and that affair was over. Or so everyone thought."

Ah, here it was.

"Well, the Dearg-Due, as it says here, is created when a woman is murdered due to some sort of tragedy, usually involving a betrayed love, and she certainly had that."

"I guess she did. What happened next?"

"First, Sweeney was haunted. He complained of boys trying to scare him, moving things in the night, howling, breaking things on his farm."

I glanced out the back window and remembered the howls.

"Then, he started getting more and more insistent that someone was trying to frighten him. No one believed him, but he grew more and more certain. And finally, he just… went mad. He ran stark naked through the street and tried to claw a visitor's eyes out."

My voice squeaked. "What… what happened to him?"

She gave a shrug. "They took him to a hospital in Dublin. No one ever heard from him again. Then the same thing started happening to Gerald."

"He was taken away, as well?"

Adanna nodded, her expression sober. "They did. The rest of that family moved away shortly thereafter."

We sat in silence for a few moments. Faelan shifted on Adanna's lap, and she stroked his back absently, still staring at the Dearg-Due drawing.

I didn't want to look at it anymore, so I kept my eyes on Adanna. "So, not to change the subject, but what does all this have to do with the things going on today?"

She raised her eyes to mine. "Don't you see? The Dearg-Due is back. That's what killed Brian."

My head started swirling again. "What? You can't possibly be serious. We're in the 21st century, aren't we? Not some ancient myth."

The doctor let out a laugh, but it was almost bitter. "You may have been here as a child, but you have a lot to learn about Ireland, Skye."

"Do you mind explaining that one?"

"I'll do something better." She pushed Faelan off her lap and got to her feet. "Let's talk out what's happened while I help you straighten up."

Fine. I was dead tired of having a messy house and needed to clean it for my own peace of mind. Especially if someone else had the key. At least Gran had added a chain inside each door. I'd definitely start using those.

Adanna grabbed the broom and began sweeping the kitchen. "So, what details do you know so far?"

"Details?"

She stopped, staring at me as if I was being deliberately obtuse. "About the murder, of course. I know you've been chasing down information all over town."

Even though I knew the answer, I asked, "Does everyone know everything around here?"

"Sure, and we've got Irish mams in every household peeking out through the curtains to see who is doing what, when, and with whom."

I would just have to get used to being the talk of the town, I guessed. "Okay, do you want to take notes while I talk it out?"

"Grand. What's the first thing?"

"Brian came into town a few days before I did, according to Seán. At least by Tuesday, though it could have been earlier. A few people had seen them together, but not the other guy."

"Do you know who the other guy is? I mean, in relation to Brian or Cherie?"

I shook my head. "No clue. I don't know if they all came together, or if he was her friend, her lover, or even Brian's lover."

"Sure and he's a mystery we need to solve. We don't even know his name?"

"Nope. You might have been the first person to see them. You saw Cherie and Brian at O'Leary's on Tuesday night, right?"

"I did. They were having a bit of a row, as I recall."

"Seán said the same thing. He also saw Cherie on the beach, arguing with the other man, Gerald. Oh, and she was wearing a bright pink scarf on Wednesday. I found a scarf on the beach."

"You found it on Wednesday?"

"No, no, on… wait, was it Thursday or Friday? Urgh!" I clutched my head in frustration."

Adanna put a hand on my arm. "Now, take a deep breath. We'll work up a timeline. So, they arrived on Tuesday. They were at O'Leary's, arguing."

"Wait, no, Seán didn't see Brian and Cherie arguing. O'Leary saw Seán and Brian arguing, on Wednesday night, not Tuesday."

She scratched something out and wrote this detail. "Got it. Then, Wednesday morning, that's when Seán saw Cherie and this other bloke at the beach?"

"Yup, arguing as well. Boy, there's lots of anger going around. Is it something in the water?" I gave a weak smile at the pathetic joke.

Adanna returned it. "And then you got into a crash. All three were there at first? I only saw Brian when I arrived."

"Cherie tried to get Brian to back down, but he was starting to get angry at her, so they ran off."

"And Seán took your car in while I took you home. That night is when Seán gets into a fight with Brian?"

I rubbed the back of my neck, sure that I was blushing. "Well, Seán was upset over Brian hitting my car, and was giving him a hard time about it."

Adanna's mouth quirked up at one corner and she gave me an appraising look. "Ah, that's our chivalric Seán. So, after that fight, Brian came to my clinic for some pain medication."

"Cherie was with him, though. Seán said she waited on the bench outside."

"Really? I didn't even see her. Okay, then…"

I swallowed back more nerves. "That's when I found Brian in my shed."

"And when someone broke into my clinic."

"Oh! I wanted to ask you something about that…"

She waggled her finger at me. "Don't get off track. We can discuss that when we're done with this timeline. So, what else happened Wednesday?"

I thought back, trying to stick events into days, but I couldn't think of much. "I did a bunch of cleaning. Then, as I was getting ready for bed..." I shuddered at the memory. It wasn't as if I hadn't seen plenty of death, but not in my own yard. "I heard something out back. Something yowling, fit to shake your bones. I went to investigate."

Adanna put her pen down and patted my arm. "And I know the rest."

Now was my best chance to ask Adanna about why she was in my garden. "You do. But I need to ask you something."

"What's that?"

I swallowed, trying to choose my words carefully. I didn't want to piss off the only real friend I'd made here. "I thought I saw you in my yard."

"Sure, and I've been here lots of times. When, in particular?"

I clenched my teeth, trying to draw up courage. "Thursday. I was going to go out and say hello, but you hurried away before I got the chance."

She furrowed her brow a moment. "Oh! Sure, I know what that was. I, uh, came to pick some garlic."

The mundane answer took me by surprise. At this point, I expected something far more exotic and magical. "Garlic? Are you serious?"

The doctor rubbed the back of her neck. "Your Gran's garlic. She promised me I could always come and pick some. I've got an incredible weakness for it, but no patience to grow things myself. You're welcome to amend that arrangement, of course."

I narrowed my eyes. Something still wasn't adding up. She had looked very cagey sneaking around that day, and now she looked like a dog who had been caught ripping up a newspaper. "That sounds super thin. What were you really doing?"

After blinking a few times in an attempt at innocence, my new friend let out a deep sigh. "Fine. But you won't believe me."

I crossed my arms, half-annoyed and half-intrigued. "Try me."

She downed the dregs of her tea and took a deep breath. "Saoirse asked me to look after… well, the wee folk."

"The *what?*"

"The wee folk. You know, the fairies? The Good Neighbors? If you don't keep them happy, they're likely to cause a great deal of mischief. Even if you don't know any better. So, I come and leave a bit of offering for them. A saucer of cream, a bit of honey, that sort of thing. I've been doing so ever since Saoirse started getting so ill."

I couldn't believe my ears. "The fairies. You were leaving treats for the fairies."

"Look, I know you don't believe me. I see it in your eyes. But you didn't believe about Faelan, either, did you?"

I jumped to my feet. "You know about Faelan?"

"Sure, and who do you think he talked to before you arrived?"

I couldn't make sense of her words and would have to think about this before accepting anything. I waved my hand. "Right, okay, let's leave that for now."

Then, she asked, "So what else happened on Thursday, after all the hubbub died down?"

"Thursday. Was that only two days ago? Right. Father Fraser came over for a chat. Then, Cormac came over and gave me some nasty threats. After that, I was about done for the night."

"Fine. Friday?"

Friday is when I found that business card and the scrap of metal. I wanted to tell Adanna, but would she tattle on me to her husband? I couldn't risk that yet. Besides, the clues were gone, stolen from my purse. I had no proof anymore. "Friday, that's when I went walking on the beach and found the pink scarf. I have that, if you want to see it."

I jumped up and pulled the bright fabric from my purse. The image of Cherie's face as she had tried to get between me and Brian made me sniff back tears. Had he hurt or killed her because of that? Was this all my fault? Maybe the Gard should be arresting me, after all.

The scarf was ripped in a few places, stained with salt water, and streaks of mud. I squinted at the mud, and just before I handed it to Adanna, I took it over to the window. In the natural light, it looked like the same mud I'd seen on the boy's sneakers. The same reddish mud I'd seen under Adanna's window.

"Where does this mud come from? I've seen it before."

She did the same as me, examining it near the window. "Mostly out on the south end of town, near the cemetery, from what I know. There might be other bits here and there."

"The cemetery. Like, near the crypt? That's where we went Saturday morning."

"Sure, that's one place. Maybe in the bog, as well."

For some reason, that made my skin prickle and I could swear some haunting music played in the back of my mind. *Yes, the bog. That's the place.* "Is that next to the cemetery, then?"

"Sure, and it's the only reason the cemetery isn't bigger."

"Interesting. Then, when I came home, I found my home had been broken into. Well, burgled. I didn't find any broken locks or windows." My gaze strayed to the chain on the door. I'd still have to get a locksmith here, and quick.

"And then went to the station?"

I couldn't keep the bitterness from my voice. "Yeah. You know what happened there. Adanna, what do you see in him?"

She pursed her lips and stared at the pen in her hands for a moment before answering. "We married when I was very young. We were both very young. I hadn't even started college yet. And he was handsome, and attentive, and my mam loved him." She let out a huge sigh. "To be fair, Dónal is sweet when we're alone. He treats me well and would be a great support if I wasn't also working."

I cocked my head. “That was phrased oddly.”

Adanna let out a humorless laugh. “He doesn’t like that I make more money than he does.”

“Damages his fragile masculinity, does it?”

She gave me a wry smile. “That must be it. Now, where were we in our timeline? We got to, uh, Friday afternoon? You walking on the beach and finding the scarf?”

“We already talked about Saturday. Us visiting the crypt and me coming home to… this.” I nodded toward the mess. My gaze lingered on a book still lying on the ground, open and face down. I ached to jump up and put it back.

“That’s it for now, then.” Adanna put the pen down with a snap and grabbed a broom. “I’ll sweep. You straighten.”

She swept the kitchen, while I picked up any unbroken items from the floor and put them in cabinets.

As we moved into the pub, she asked, “So, has anyone but you and Seán seen this Gerald? The thin one?” I grabbed the mop, as some of the broken bottles had still contained liquor. The place reeked of alcohol.

I shook my head. “Not that I’ve been able to tell. Cherie went off with him before everyone else showed up to my accident.” That made it sound like I’d been throwing a party or something. “Unless your network of Irish mams noticed anything?”

She let out a chuckle. “Not so much that they’ve said, but I can have an ask around.”

We worked out a few more details before she glanced at her watch. "I've got to run. We can talk more later, aye? Why don't you meet me at O'Leary's?"

Yay. My favorite place in the world. *Not.*

CHAPTER FIFTEEN

Once Adanna left, I finished sweeping up the broken glass in the pub. I was just about to dump the dustpan in the trash bin when I noticed some fabric amidst the debris. I examined the scrap of denim.

So, whoever had broken in had been wearing jeans. Ripped jeans, now. I tucked the scrap into my purse. Then, thinking better of it, I shoved it into the little zipper pocket in the bottom to make it harder to find.

I looked around to ensure everything was in place once more. I felt so much better after cleaning up, I realized a great deal of my stress today was simply from the house being messy. Armand always got angry when he found a mess, so I'm sure that had a lot to do with my anxiety.

I'd worked up a sweat with the cleaning, so I ran upstairs for a quick wash and change of clothes. If Adanna was going to meet me at O'Leary's, I could head over there now. Maybe I could find out some more information about who was harassing me, or at least who else might have a key to this place.

Besides, I hadn't yet gone to the pub for a pint. Isn't that what one does in Ireland, of an evening?

Before I left, I slid the diary between two books of the same color. I pursed my lips as I surveyed the shelf, satisfied that it blended well.

I couldn't lock the chain from the outside, but I wouldn't leave the most valuable thing in here in plain sight.

I was keenly conscious of locking the door behind me. My skin crawled as if someone was watching me. It was just dusk, but something was creeping me out. This had been a very long day, and I could use a drink and some people around me.

The road in front of Gran's house was unnaturally quiet. Not even the night birds were singing yet. I'd always enjoyed that liminal time, halfway between day and night, a time when anything might happen. A time when the veil between worlds might be thin.

Now I was thinking like Adanna, seeing supernatural beings behind every creak and sigh. When the wind howled, I shuddered. Not quite the banshee wail, but close enough that logic and science felt far away from this town.

I hurried down the street and around to the much brighter-lit main street. O'Leary's was bright and welcoming and filled with people. Most importantly, it looked safe.

While I'd visited once already, that was in the daytime, when the place wasn't open yet. Now, the place was filled with people. Some sat at tables, with sandwiches or soup in front of them. More sat at the bar, nursing pints. Everyone was talking or laughing, and the sheer volume of the place almost pushed me back out the door.

O'Leary was behind the bar, chatting with a couple of his patrons. He looked happy, charming, and relaxed. Adanna had mentioned he'd been raking it in, since Gran closed down O'Shea's, and the evidence of that was right before my eyes.

Once again, the notion that O'Leary was behind my harassment pushed to the front of my mind. I'd just about had enough of being frightened, whether by O'Leary, a Dearg-Due, a banshee, juvenile delinquents, or dead men in my shed. It was time to get to the bottom of all this.

I spied Seán at one end of the bar, sitting next to the youngish woman with the wild red-blond hair I'd seen earlier, as well as Joshua from the café and another woman, presumably his wife. I didn't remember her name, though. Just past Seán was an older man, drinking alone. He seemed to be muttering something, but no one was listening.

A raucous laugh pierced my skull and I turned to find the source. The noise came from a rather short man, middle-aged, with weathered skin. He wore a grimy t-shirt and jeans. I peered at his jeans closely, but I couldn't see any rips.

The discordant screech of a fiddle being tuned drew my attention to the far-right corner, near the bathrooms. Three men and a woman sat around a round table. Two held fiddles, one was cleaning a tin whistle, and the woman held a bodhrán, the small hand-drum the Irish used. It seemed we'd have some music soon.

Gran had tried to teach me the tin whistle when I was a child. It had taken me weeks just to play 'hot cross buns' and I'd given it up as a bad job. Now, I regretted the decision, as being unmusical in Ireland was practically a crime. Maybe I could take some classes. The fiddle took actual skill, though. Did I have the breath control for the tin whistle? Maybe the bodhrán would be easier.

"What'll you have, Miss O'Shea?"

O'Leary's voice cut through my mind-fog, and I gave him a polite smile as I stepped up to the bar. "A pint of cider, please. Do you have a moment to chat?"

His smile slipped a notch, then he burst out with a laugh that rivaled the earlier one. "Does it look like I've got a moment to chat, darlin'? Some of us have to work for a living. Isn't that right, Ciaran?" O'Leary turned to the man who had been laughing. Startled, the other man just lifted his pint in a salute and went back talking to the woman next to him.

"Right. Well, even if you don't have time, I have some questions for you."

Now, O'Leary scowled. "You'll have to wait. Come back in the morning."

I didn't want to come back in the morning. I certainly didn't want to try to sleep tonight, knowing someone might try to get back into my house. I used my nurse voice and it carried. "Do you have a set of keys to my pub?"

The musicians in the corner launched into a sprightly tune and most folks fell silent to listen. O'Leary stared at me, his scowl growing deeper with every second.

I raised my eyebrows, refusing to give an inch.

"Now, why would Saoirse give me keys to her pub? Sure and she never wanted me near the place."

The music had jangled to a halt, and my voice cut clear across the silence. "Someone's been trying to frighten me away from this town ever since I got here. You have the most to gain from my pub never opening again. Can you deny that?"

Not one person so much as moved a muscle as we stared each other down.

In a quiet tone, O'Leary said, "You had better be certain of your facts before you go around slinging accusations."

The door to the pub jingled open. Adanna came in, and I almost sighed with relief. Then her husband, Dónal McCarthy, came in behind her. I almost didn't recognize him out of his Gard uniform, but there he was. He didn't look any more relaxed in civvies than he did in his crisp uniform.

I glanced back at O'Leary, and then to Gard McCarthy. If he realized I was asking questions again, he could justify calling immigration. I could say goodbye to the house, the pub, and this whole new life.

My breath caught, and I decided that wisdom was the better part of valor. "I'll come back tomorrow, Mr. O'Leary. Have a lovely evening."

Then, I hightailed it out of there, away from the glitzy lights and into the dark night. I would just have to meet Adanna another time.

An echo of laughter faded behind me.

As soon as I was back in the cool, crisp evening air, I could breathe more easily. It took a moment before my heart calmed, though. I rested on a bench just outside the pub. For a moment, I felt utterly alone in this town. Everyone was inside, having a lovely Saturday evening, while I was an outsider, excluded and lonely.

Well, that was my fault, wasn't it? I was the one going around playing detective, asking people where they were, what they were doing, and sticking my nose into everything. What else could I have done? The man had been killed on my property. With the Gard being such a jerk, I had to do something.

After pushing myself off the bench, I began to walk down the street and back to my road. Voices came from far behind me. I turned, in case it was McCarthy trying to grab me and put me into jail again, but it was those same boys heading into the corner store.

Was Máiréad's shop still open? She'd closed at 6 pm the other night. Maybe she stayed open longer on Saturdays.

Thinking of the scrap of denim from the pub, I marched toward the shop. I wanted to see if any of these roughs had ripped jeans.

I pulled the door open and the doorbell chimed. Máiréad glanced up, and relief colored her expression. The boys were clustered around the register, and it looked like I'd interrupted something tense.

Well, I had no problem acting the heavy. How dare these boys attack an old woman? "Good evening, Máiréad. I'm surprised you're open this late."

"And a lovely evening to you, Miss O'Shea. I was just closing up when these young men came in."

I stared at the tallest one, who looked like the leader, while surreptitiously studying his pants, searching for rips. I didn't see any. "Aren't you a bit old to be buying candy bars for your mates?"

He growled. "This ain't none of your business, lady. Clear off."

For some reason, while they'd frightened me earlier, this time the boys didn't make me nervous. I was more in control now. "No, I don't think I will. I think you should all leave and let the shopkeeper close up, as she wishes."

We locked gazes for several moments. The others watched him, waiting for his move I put steel into my gaze, like when ordering interns around. Finally, he dropped his eyes and shuffled out with a desultory, "C'mon."

They all filed out behind him like leather-jacket clad ducklings. As each one passed, I searched for rips in their jeans, but they were all clean. Well, not clean. There were stains and dirt and… Wait. One had reddish dirt on his jeans and his shoes, like I'd seen under Adanna's window after her break-in.

Could they have stolen from her clinic? And my pub? Or was this just coincidence? A motive for the clinic was easy enough, but why would these kids care about my pub? Other than a few broken bottles, there wasn't much alcohol missing.

I was going to make them stop, but I should let them leave, so Máiréad could close up in peace. I turned to the older woman. "Are you alright? Did they do anything?"

She waved a hand, but I could tell she was nervous. "Oh, no, they didn't do a thing. They might have, though. Thank you for coming by when you did."

Just in case, I escorted her back to her house, which was just a few houses down on the side street. Then, I returned to the main street, but I didn't want to go back to my house. Besides the fact that I didn't feel safe there, the mud on that kid's jeans and shoes was niggling at me.

Not expecting to find anything, I hurried down to Adanna's clinic and, using my phone flashlight, tried to find the mud. As I suspected, there was nothing there. Rain must have washed it away.

Maybe someone knew where that reddish mud came from. With my luck, it was everywhere. Perhaps I was wrong.

Just as I passed back toward O'Leary's, Adanna stuck her head out the door. "Skye! I thought we were meeting for a pint?"

I didn't want to be there if McCarthy was, but I did promise her a drink. Besides, I had to face him sometime. This was a small town, and I couldn't hide from him forever.

Once more unto the breach.

With a friend by my side, it didn't feel nearly as scary. I'd never been a social butterfly and tended to be a permanent wallflower. However, with Adanna to help, I was introduced to the entire town, table by table, so it seemed.

We got a couple of ciders and started at the far end. "Now, this old gent is Pádraig O'Sullivan. He runs a sheep farm along the shore down on the south end of town."

I put out my hand to shake, but he just lifted his Guinness as a salute, mumbled something utterly incomprehensible, and turned back to the bar. I had no idea if he was speaking English or Irish.

Adanna let out a chuckle. "Pay him no mind, Skye. He's mostly harmless. Now Seán, you've met."

We exchanged a pleasant nod, and I was glad the lights were dim, so he wouldn't notice my flushed face. Must be the cider.

"And this bright ray of summer sun is Jess Murphy. She runs a wee art gallery along the main street." I turned to see the woman with red-blond hair I kept seeing, the one who seemed to glow with yellow light. Not now, of course. There was no sunshine in the pub.

"Welcome to Ballybás, Skye! I'll have to come over with a basket of goodies for you soon."

"That's so kind of you, Jess."

Then Adanna moved us down to the next group. I met Finn and Rory Lynch, the cousins Seán was telling me about. One was blond and lanky, wearing a well-faded baseball cap, while the other was shorter, with dark hair and a flannel shirt.

After that, all the names and faces were a blur. Not helped, I was certain, by the cider. I was such a lightweight that just the one pint made my head buzz.

"Can we find a place to sit, Adanna? It's been a very long day."

After a couple of pints, my face was dripping with sweat. I turned to my friend. "Adanna! I need to get some air."

I abandoned her and once outside, sucked in the fresh, cool May air. There was still a hint of light on the horizon, so it wasn't as late as I thought. Then I reminded myself that days grew very long in the Irish summer. A glance at my phone proved that it was almost ten.

I'd have to re-learn the pattern of the seasons here. This area was as far north as Newfoundland, despite the mild weather.

A howl filled the air. The same sort of howl I'd heard before, and it ran up and down my spine, making my skin crawl.

"Skye? Are you unwell?" Adanna came out and put her arm around my shoulder.

"Did you hear it?"

"Hear what?" Then it yowled again. She waved her hand in dismissal. "Oh. It seems the banshee is on the prowl tonight."

"Or the Dearg-Due."

"It could be any of the Fair Folk, Skye, to be sure. We don't want to be out on a night when they're abroad. Come back inside."

She tugged at my arm, but I resisted. "No, I need to go find it."

"What? Skye, have you lost your wits? This isn't a time to be out in the dark."

I glared at my new friend and planted my feet wide. "Adanna, I've been afraid most of my adult life. Of people, of situations, of new things. When I moved here, I swore I'd be braver. I promised myself I'd no longer let fear rule me. I need to figure out what the heck this thing is, and why it's following me. Or trying to scare me out of my mind."

She put her fists on her hips and gave me a narrow look. "And how do you propose to do this?"

I glanced down the street toward the church and the cemetery. "That mud on Cherie's scarf? That came from the cemetery. There was a bit under your window after the break-in, too. And on those rough gang's jeans. At least one of them. I mean to go find who it is. I'll bet you dollars to donuts that it's a human, not a fairy."

Adanna pursed her lips. "Don't call them that, aye? Use Fair Folk or Good Folk. It's safer. If you're headed to that blasted cemetery, I guess I'll have to come, too. There's no way on God's green earth that I'd let you go there alone on a night like this. As long as you don't take me into the bog!"

I didn't have it in me to argue at that moment. To be honest, her presence made me feel a lot less frightened.

We both remained silent as we walked down the street. The last streetlamp faded behind us as we passed the dark, silent church. Wind made the trees sough and the hairs on my arms stood on end. I could smell just a hint of the sea, as well as earth and leaves and summer.

Of course, when we opened the gate, it creaked like something straight out of a Hallowe'en movie. Mist had already started to form, hugging the hills and the graves. We followed the path to my family's crypt. Just as we arrived, another howl pierced the silence.

I grabbed Adanna's hand, and she squeezed back.

After taking out my phone, I flicked the light on and examined the mud near the crypt entrance. Then I took out Cherie's scarf and held it close. "See? Here, that's the same color mud. It's dried but looks just like the scarf."

But then I realized it wasn't quite like the mud on the gang's shoes, and my hopes fell. Maybe I wasn't such a clever detective after all.

Adanna placed a hand on the crypt door. "Skye? Did you come here later and go inside?"

"No, I don't even have the key." Then I remembered that ring of old keys. "Or, if I do, I don't know it. Why? What do you see?"

"Someone's been inside here. Or opened the door. Recently, too, judging from the fresh gouge on this door."

I bent to examine the scratches, shining my phone light on it. The weathered, dark wood was marred by bright, new wood. Definitely a recent injury.

Adanna's eyes were wide as they met mine. "We should fetch Dónal."

I shook my head. "No, he'll just try to arrest me again for wasting police time."

"Skye, about that… I'm sorry he's being such a jerk."

"Yeah, so am I. What's his deal, anyhow?"

She stared toward the village for a few moments before answering. "There was this thing with your grandfather and his Da. I don't know all the details, but it was a huge thing for many years."

"Oh, great. So, it *is* some mafia-like family vendetta. And I'm paying the price for something my grandfather did? A grandfather I never even met?"

"That's all I know, sorry. It might take some time before he gives you a chance."

"Right. Well, that just solidifies my opinion that he'll be no help. Besides, waiting for him to join us will give whoever did this too much time to get away. If they've been watching me, like I suspect they have, then they might just come in and erase any clues while we're gone."

"You aren't being smart, Skye! This isn't some game. Even if there's a human at work, you could get hurt."

I furrowed my brow. "Even if it's a human? Are you seriously thinking there's something nonhuman at work?"

She stared straight into my eyes. "The Fair Folk exist, and I have no doubt about that. I have seen them. I've heard them." The doctor shuddered. "I've had to deal with them, and it's no mean feat to escape from such a deal unscathed."

I couldn't digest that bit of information. "You go get your husband. I'll stay here and guard the crypt."

She stared at the door and back at me. "I'll call him."

As she pulled out her phone and held it to her ear, wind blew through the trees, bringing on a new chill. I couldn't tell if the wind was howling or something else. Adanna frowned, staring at her phone screen. "He's not answering, and that's not like him."

I drew my finger along the gouge and said quietly, "Go get him. Come back quickly."

The moon was just beginning to rise, a sliver of silver on the horizon, making the sky glow indigo. As Adanna disappeared into the gloom, I rubbed the skin on my arms.

I should have waited for them, but bent to re-examine the scratches. They were definitely fresh, rectangular, and deep, and not made by a person. At least, not by someone's hand. It looked like some sort of box or table corner hit it.

Had someone brought something into the crypt? If I waited for the Gard to arrive, he probably wouldn't allow me into my family's crypt. Worse, he might hide clues. I had lost all faith in his integrity as an officer.

It was a horrible idea, but I had to look inside. I'd never been the sharpest knife in the box.

After glancing over my shoulder to see if Adanna had miraculously reappeared with Gard McCarthy already, I depressed the old-fashioned door latch.

A sudden, bone-chilling gust of wind swept around me, and my hands began to shake as the crypt door opened with an ear-splitting creak.

CHAPTER SIXTEEN

Pitch black greeted me. I fumbled with my phone and shone inside. A sleeping bag was neatly rolled in one corner, along with a pillow. And a pair of jeans, muddy and ripped. Which meant whoever was sleeping here must have broken into my pub.

I let out a sigh. Not the Fair Folk, after all. The stink of chemicals, blood, and something rotten hit me.

As I stepped inside, my phone light glinted on a jumble of metal and glass things peeking out from under the ripped jeans. With a shock, I recognized them. Some broken medicine vials, an arterial tube, a draining tube, and a pump. Three syringes, one with a broken needle. So, this must also be who robbed Adanna's clinic.

All the things someone would need to drain the blood from a body in an embalming. And they'd dropped some of this equipment in my garden.

Which meant there was no Dearg-Due. Someone had gone to a great deal of trouble to pretend to be one. Or to convince me that there was one.

Why would anyone want to do that? The most obvious answer was to deflect suspicion from themselves. But why this way? Surely, there were easier ways to shift focus.

Whoever did this must have some reason to use this particular legend. Then I remembered that someone had opened Gran's diary to that page. That was after I found the victim drained of blood.

Suddenly, the stench of the crypt overcame me. I needed to escape before I was sick. As soon as I stepped outside, back into the cool, fresh wind, my nausea eased.

Someone coughed behind me.

I spun, flashing my phone into the darkening mist. A howl echoed across the cemetery, and I fought the urge to flee. Why would a fairy cough? Whoever was there had to be human. Nevertheless, I wished Adanna and her husband would hurry up and get back here. "Who's out there? Show yourself!"

Rustling bushes were my only answer. They were going away from me. "Wait! Get back here!"

I was torn. Should I follow whoever had obviously been watching me? The howl sounded again, from another direction. Maybe there was something else at play here, other than the person camping in the crypt.

No, I had to find them. I had to prove myself to Gran. I rushed in the direction of the rustling, using my phone to scan the ground in front of me. Despite that, roots and bracken tripped me several times.

I stopped, trying to hear where they were. To the left! I moved in that direction and tripped on a root, falling flat on my face. The loamy scent of rotting vegetation filled my nose.

Muttering under my breath, "Sheep nuggets!" I pushed myself to my feet, and everything was pitch dark. I couldn't find my phone, so it must have fallen face down. Feeling around the leaf mold and grass, I found it and shone it around me. Nothing moved but the wind. Not even a howl from the resident ghoul.

I lost him.

No, something was behind me. I whirled, only to find a huge black cat. "Faelan? What are you doing here?"

He stalked past me and then stopped at the edge of the clearing and glanced back. "What do you think I'm doing, human? I'm showing you where your quarry fled to."

"Oh, you're talking again?"

He growled, "Will you talk, or will you follow?"

"Fine! Show me where."

And so, I followed a fairy cat through a dark, foggy cemetery in the middle of the night in a town I barely knew.

I crawled through breaks in the bracken and ducked under drooping branches. A few times, I stubbed my toe on roots or lumps, despite my phone's light. Our steps were punctuated with howls, both from the wind and whatever was trying to frighten me, be it human or fairy.

I lost track of how long we crept through the cemetery. Surely, it wasn't this big? But there was a forest beyond the graves, and we must be well into that.

The mist grew thicker, and I could barely see the cat. My phone's light was almost worse than nothing, as the fog dispersed it, making the entire area glow. My footsteps squished now and then, and I was worried we'd wandered into the bog.

Faelan halted, his tail twitching.

I glanced around. We were in another clearing, but not a big one. The ground was beginning to squelch under my feet, and I remembered the cemetery was hemmed in by a bog. I had no idea "Which way?"

The cat turned around and opened his mouth, but nothing came out.

"Really? *Now* is when you decide to go silent?"

Maybe he couldn't always talk? Or maybe the fairy cat just didn't know where the other person went. Come to think about it, I had no idea where we were now in relation to the crypt, the church, or even the town. Somewhere in the distance, waves lapped the shore, but the wind kept blowing and I couldn't tell the direction of the ocean.

Then Faelan darted off again, and I grumbled as I followed him.

Howling swirled around my head, making me shiver so hard, my bones hurt.

A shriek ripped through the darkness, and I halted, my eyes darting around. Where was it? What was it? The banshee wails pressed in on me, a solid wall of terror. I covered my ears and ducked my head, trying to escape the terror.

Flashes of sickly green light popped all around me, and I fell to my knees.

This is it. This is how I die, all alone in a freezing bog.

Then, a scrap of haunting melody blanked out the fear and then, the screams stopped. Gran's warm arms hugged me tight until everything fell utterly still and silent.

Had Gran just saved me from the Dearg-Due? I couldn't think of what else it could have been.

Something moved in the underbrush, and Faelan's glowing eyes blinked at me. He darted away, and I followed with a shudder. Maybe it was Gran and Faelan working together. Whatever had saved me, my heart was thankful.

After a few more moments of pushing through bushes, thorns tearing at my clothing and exposed skin, we burst upon another clearing.

A man stood in the middle of the space, fumbling at something on his belt. He drew out a long, wicked knife. With a cold certainty, I recognized the guy from Brian's car, the one who had run off with Cherie. Gerald.

Smears of blood painted his white shirt.

His eyes were darting back and forth, desperation clear in his expression. I held out my hands, though that was awkward while shining my phone on him. "Don't worry. I'm not here to hurt you. I remember seeing you the day I came to town. You were with Cherie, right? What's your name?"

It was a mistake to mention Cherie. When I did, he let out a howl, so much like the ones I'd been hearing, I was certain he was the source. But there had been other howls, in other directions. Another echoed in the night, perhaps in answer to his rage. Maybe I wasn't as certain as I thought.

"Please, I'm here to help. I'm a nurse. You trust nurses, right? We only want to help people to heal."

He was panting, his wide eyes darting from side to side. Very little humanity remained in his gaze, and I hoped I wasn't too late to bring him back from the brink of madness.

Slowly, I placed my phone on the ground, shining up. That way, it wasn't directly in his eyes, but it might be a beacon to Adanna and Dónal. "What's your name?"

The other man shrank back, then mumbled something.

"I'm sorry, can you speak just a bit louder? The wind is making it hard to hear you." My nurse training kicked in and I needed to get him talking. Calm and conversational.

His voice wavered and cracked as he said, "Gerald. I'm Gerald."

I nodded my head, giving my best nurse smile, reserved for the most frightened children. Those about to go into a major surgery, holding onto their last scrap of hope with fierce, clutching, tiny hands. "My name is Skye. I'm very pleased to meet you, Gerald."

Gerald's breathing slowed. His muscles were still incredibly tense, and he stood in a fighting stance, a crouch ready to grapple, that wicked knife gripped in his right hand. The thing must be at least a foot long and was obviously sharp. I kept an eye on it as I spoke. "Are you from this area, Gerald?"

That wasn't the right thing to ask. He yowled and whimpered and curled up into a ball, rocking as he sobbed. I wanted to come close and get the knife away from him, but he was too unpredictable to dare.

I glanced behind me, hoping Adanna would come soon. Hoping she could see the phone flashlight shining up into the sky. A very faint glow hit the clouds.

If Cherie had caused such a reaction from him, I didn't dare ask about Brian. Still, I had a few ideas. This wasn't my first encounter with frightened people. "Is there anything I can do to make you feel safer?"

Gerald stopped rocking, and I took one careful step closer. A twig snapped beneath my weight, and his head whipped up. "Go away! Don't touch me!"

"It's alright, Gerald. I won't touch you. I'll stay over here. Can you tell me what you're frightened of?"

He stared at me, his gaze piercing my soul. "Cherie. Cherie's gone."

I swallowed and asked, "Where did Cherie go, Gerald?"

He began rocking again. "She's gone! She's gone she's gone she's gone. It's all his fault."

I kept my voice as calm and comforting as I could. "Whose fault is it, Gerald?"

CHAPTER SEVENTEEN

Mist caressed the terrified young man as he leapt from his ball of misery and scrambled to the edge of the clearing, still gripping the knife. "Brian did it. Brian did it. She's dead and Brian did it!"

A sneaking suspicion crept into my mind. "Shh, shh, Gerald. Can you tell me where it started? How do you know Brian?"

"Brian did it!"

I gave a nod and put my hands out. "Yes, I believe you. When did you meet Brian?"

He bent over in a feral pose and mumbled. "Dublin. We were in Dublin."

I tried to see what happened to the knife. Was he still clutching it? Had he dropped it? "Can you tell me what happened in Dublin?"

He let out a yip and a howl, but finally gave me an answer. "He met her. He met her at a pub and gave her a drink. I told her not to, but she did. And she liked him and he liked her, but I didn't like him. I told her not to like him."

So, Gerald must have been out with Cherie when Brian bought her a drink. Was Gerald dating her? "Is Cherie your girlfriend, Gerald?"

He balled his fists and shook them up and down, like a child in a tantrum. "No! No! No!"

"She isn't your girlfriend? Is she your friend? Your sister?"

"Sister. She's my sister. My little sister. Protect her, Da said. Keep her safe. Keep her safe."

And if she was dead, as I suspected, and that Brian had killed her, then he had failed. "So, Brian brought her here from Dublin?"

"He took her but she wouldn't go without me and I didn't want to go and he tried to do things with her and she didn't want to…" He let out a mighty howl, then fell into a sobbing pile again.

Ah. "And where is Cherie now?"

"I took her away. I took her from him and hid her where he couldn't find her and he'd never find her. But he found me and her, and then he hurt me and her and I had to run away. But I finally found him!" Gerald looked up at me, his eyes glinting in eager joy. "I found him. And she was with me when I found him and we took care of him. And now he will never find her again!"

I tried to wrap my mind around the flood of pronouns. He was giving more complete sentences, at least, so maybe I was helping to call him. But he still seemed on the edge of madness.

So, Gerald had killed Brian for hurting his sister. An understandable reaction, though still a murder. Could Cherie still be alive somewhere? Gerald said Brian *took her away.* That could mean many things, but I doubted it.

But why would Gerald drain Brian's blood? And how? "Gerald… what did you do to Brian?"

Dead silence fell across the clearing. Mist swirled in the phone's light, and I hoped that would make the beacon easier to find. Not that I had a huge hope that they could see it from anywhere, with all the trees.

"I took his blood. Cherie told me to take his blood. My Da took blood. That was his job."

What in the name of God's green earth did his father do? "Was your dad a nurse?"

"No, no, after the nurse. After the doctor. After the death."

After the death. His father must have worked in a mortuary, and embalmed people. Then I remembered the bent metal stick that I found next to the Dead Shed, and things snapped into place. "But why did you drain Brian's blood?"

He shook his head so fast, I thought he'd snap his neck. "I didn't. The Dearg-Due took it. Cherie is the Dearg-Due. She took Brian's blood. She used my hands, but she took it. My grandfa told me of the Dearg-Due. It haunted him. Now Cherie will haunt Brian. *She* took Brian's blood. But she won't leave me alone now. She's there, she's always there. She'll always be there."

Wow. Okay, that was some convoluted logic. Did the Dearg-Due possess Gerald when he murdered Brian and drained his blood? A shudder danced up my spine.

Then, I remembered Adanna's story about my grandfather, Sweeney O'Shea. And the name of the man whose wife he'd taken, Gerald Brennan. Surely, this was a coincidence?

"Gerald? Was your grandfather named Gerald, too? Gerald Brennan?"

His sobbing stopped and he stared straight into my eyes again. For one shining moment, he seemed utterly sane. "He was my grandfather. But he was betrayed! Sweeney did it. He made the first Dearg-Due by killing my grandmother." His glare deepened into something quite mad, though his words sounded calmer. "Your grandfather. Your family. And when Cherie became a Dearg-Due and used my hands, I had to leave the body on your land. That completes the circle."

A sound rode the wind. Not an unearthly howl, but human voices shouting. Did I dare yell back? I glanced at Gerald, who had hunched over again, mumbling about Cherie and the Dearg-Due drinking all the blood. About sixteen chills ran down my spine, and I took a step backward.

I snuck a quick look at my phone, still shining into the sky. I darted down to grab it, and stood straight again, balancing on the balls of my feet to run if I had to. Gerald either didn't notice or didn't care.

Shielding the phone with my body, I held it behind my back and tilted it back and forth, making the light move in the mist. It looked like subliminal flashing, as if there was weak lightning darting through the fog.

Someone shouted again. A man's voice. Gerald didn't move, though his gaze darted into the darkness several times.

My heart raced and I ached to call out, but he was still too close to me. If he leapt out of his crouch, he could be on me with that knife before I could even turn around and get out of the clearing.

I took another step backwards, slowly, slowly, no sudden movements. If I had to run, I'd probably drop my phone, so carefully, slowly, I tucked it into my bra.

Then, something cracked, and Gerald's head snapped up. He let out a mighty snarl. "You can't go away! You'll tell everyone! There's one more thing left to close the circle."

He lunged at me.

CHAPTER EIGHTEEN

In the near-darkness, I zagged to the left, but he still caught my ankle. A scream escaped my frozen throat. I let out a barely audible squeak and sucked in a deep breath.

Something stirred in the bushes, and my heart burst with hope. Kicking my leg, I managed to get free of his grasp and scrambled away on all fours toward the edge of the clearing. He gave a howling cry. The sound echoed through the misty forest and panic made my heart jump into my throat, but I would not let this man hurt me.

When I looked up, the clearing was empty.

"Adanna? Are you out there?"

Everything was silent except my pounding heart. Was someone else near? Or something? I didn't want to think about the types of creatures I'd meet in a dark, misty night, on the edge of a bog in rural Ireland. At least the moon had come out, still almost full and pretty bright. A few clouds filtered the light into a soft glow.

I needed to find my way back to civilization. Belatedly, I patted my bra to ensure that my phone was still there. Back to the church, the cemetery, the crypt. That's where Adanna said she'd bring everyone.

With my back against a gnarly oak, I held my breath and listened. Nothing but a breeze whispering through the trees. Gerald must be gone. I let out my breath with a shudder and pulled up the map on my phone, then punched in the church name. That should get me to safety.

My power was down to 3%.

Fantastic.

Well, best use it while I had it. The flashlight would make it drain faster, but I absolutely needed the help, or I'd trip over a tree root and drown in the bog.

I started in the right direction, but the map ignored land features. I was blocked by a huge hillock of thick brush and had to skirt around it. Then, there was a soft section, and I had to test each step before I put my weight down.

The power dropped to 2%.

A huge fallen tree, rotting away with age, blocked my progress, and the ground to the right was pure swamp, so I went around to the left. Despite the light, I tripped on a thin root and dropped my phone. After I brushed myself off, I had to search for the phone.

1%. I hoped I was getting close. I stopped to listen for a moment but heard nothing but the wind through the trees and some singing frogs. I didn't know if that was good or bad.

Something brushed my leg, and I jumped back, letting out a shout of panic. When I shone my light, it was an enormous black cat.

"Faelan! Am I glad to see you. Can you get me back to the crypt? My phone is almost dead."

"*Mrow.* Of course, I can. Cat eyesight is far superior to pathetic human abilities. And you *are* in the place of the dead, after all."

I just wanted to be safe in a place that wasn't a dark bog on a dark night. "Do you know where Adanna is?"

He ignored my question and wound through several paths, but I had no idea what criteria he used to choose his direction. My phone grew dim and the light died. However, the moon had shed its cloudy shroud and shone bright on the ground. Even so, I tripped and stumbled a lot as moonlight distorted the obstacles.

We passed a gravestone. Then another. As we came into a clear space, I let out a huge sigh of relief as the crypt was right in front of us.

Faelan looked up at me, and his eyes glowed in the moonlight. "You will be safe now."

Then he disappeared, and I stepped in a hole. Once again, I fell flat on my face. Once again, I was spitting out leaf mold and muck.

Someone called out, "Where are you?" It sounded like Gard McCarthy.

I shouted, "Over here!"

Picking myself up from the ground, I brushed off the leaves and dirt that had traveled with me through the bog and scrubbed at my face. Four people burst into the clearing: McCarthy, Adanna, Seán, and Cormac.

Adanna stared at the open crypt door. "What happened?"

I took a deep breath and said, "There's a man running away right now. His name is Gerald. Tall, thin, blond hair. Absolutely out of his mind with grief. I think Brian killed his sister, Cherie, so he killed Brian."

McCarthy, Seán, and Cormac exchanged glances. The Gard asked, "Which way did he run?"

"I don't know. I went into the crypt and saw his stuff. Then something rustled outside. I chased him through the forest and into the bog." I couldn't help a shudder as the wind blew.

Sean took off his coat and wrapped it around my shoulders. I gave him tired but grateful smile, and wished I had enough courage to ask him about that red-headed woman in the photo. But now wasn't the time for all that.

Adanna drew her breath sharply. "You could have gotten lost out there! Or killed!"

"I realize that, now. But I got him to talk, at least. He's frightened, armed with a long knife, and out in the bog somewhere."

Adanna turned to her husband. "Gather a search party. We'll find him. You," she turned to me, "Home. Now. I say this as your doctor."

Numbly, I let Adanna lead me home. I craved the lights and warmth of the village. Once inside the pub, I left my now useless phone, but grabbed my actual flashlight instead.

With her hands on her hips, Adanna glared at me. "Where do you think you're off to now?"

"I need to help find Gerald."

"You need to do no such thing, ya pure eejit! What you need is rest and a hot bath, like."

"No, Adanna. I've got to do this. I owe it to everyone. I owe it to Gran."

"What are you talking about?"

I swallowed. "It's the only way I'll prove that I'm part of the community. That I'm worthy to follow in Gran's footsteps."

She scowled but after a few more moments, gave me a quick nod. "Fine. As soon as we find him, you're to come back here!"

Many folks in the village gathered around. I recognized Finn and Rory, Joshua, Father Fraser, and Ciaran. There were a few others I didn't know, but we could use all the help we could get.

Each came armed with flashlights and McCarthy handed out walkie-talkies to each searcher. "Right, this man is armed and presumed unstable." He sent me a glare, but I lifted my chin. If he'd believed me in the first place, we wouldn't be here.

I said, "His name is Gerald, and I believe his last name is Brennan. His grandfather lived here. Brian hurt his sister, and she might be out there, too. I have no idea if she's alive or dead. Gerald wasn't making much sense."

McCarthy organized everyone in groups of three and paired me with Father Fraser and Cormac. The Gard raised his voice again as he handed us our walkie-talkie. "Don't be a hero. If you find him, call in, and we'll come to you. Keep hidden if you can, but if you can't, do your best to calm him until we can arrive."

Then he gave each of us a direction to search in. He sent me, Cormac and the Father along the edge of the forest toward the beach. It was a different direction from where I'd encountered Gerald, but to tell the truth, I wasn't eager to be the one who found him. My earlier courage seems to have fled with my adrenaline. I'd had enough of madness this night.

Cormac had the strongest flashlight, some industrial sized one, with LED lights. He took point without even asking, but I was happy for someone else to take the lead. I was still sort of shaking from my encounter.

"Keep close behind me, and if you hear anything, let me know, and I'll stop so we can investigate."

At least he wasn't being a jerk at the moment, and I'd take what little wins I could get. Another blast of wind made me pull my coat—Sean's coat—tighter.

We trudged back and forth through the woods, shining our light into hollows and fallen trees, brambles and clearings. The priest seemed to jump at every sound. Every twig or branch or bird taking flight startled him. For once, though, I was calmer. I hated to admit it, but I felt safer with men around me.

Something glowed in the darkness to the right. I touched Cormac's shoulder, and he stopped walking. Father Fraser joined us as we all peered into the night.

The priest whispered, "Is that metal? The moon shining on it?"

I gave a shrug. "I think it's the wrong angle."

Cormac hefted his flashlight. "Stay here. I'll go look."

I grabbed his shoulder. "Like hell you will!"

The father sighed. "Please, Miss O'Shea."

I rolled my eyes, knowing none of them would see that. "We stick together, right?"

But Cormac was already striding off the path. I glanced back at the priest, but he wasn't budging.

Rustling to my left made me look, and then something tackled me in the middle, and I went down. I struggled against whatever it was. Images of mythological creatures flashed through my mind as I grunted and tried to push it off me. Arms locked around my neck, and I struggled to breathe. I kicked up and was rewarded with a sharp cry. So, it *could* be hurt. That meant my attacker was probably a human.

Then, the weight was gone. I looked up and saw Cormac and Father Fraser holding Gerald.

Gerald screeched out and shouted, "No! No! You can't stop the Dearg-Due! The Dearg-Due will haunt you to the end of time!"

I took in a shuddering breath and reminded myself he was having a psychotic break, not casting an evil curse. I hoped.

As my heart stopped racing, I pressed the button on the walkie-talkie. "We've got him."

CHAPTER NINETEEN

My panic faded into fatigue as everyone scrambled around me. While Father Fraser was no kind of fighting man, Cormac was solid enough to keep a good hold on Gerald while I guided the others to our location via the walkie-talkies.

I didn't understand why he had attacked me, unless he believed I'd betrayed him. I suppose, in a way, I did. I told the police about what he did. The nurse in me realized that he did need help, and I did the right thing getting him into custody, even if he hadn't committed murder.

He was mumbling to himself, and while I mostly ignored it, he spoke Cherie's name. Using my gentle nurse voice, I asked, "Cherie? Do you know where she is, Gerald?"

Gerald continued mumbling, but his eyes darted up now and then, as if searching for something. If she was out there, somewhere, alive or dead, we needed to find her. Either to rescue her… or to give her a proper burial.

While I had no wish to make Gerald's mental prison worse, I had to find his sister. For his sake, if not her own. In a way, I suppose, I was responsible, since it was my accident that caused them to run away from Brian on Wednesday. That may have been just one of several incidents that led to the murder, but every straw is an extra weight on the donkey's back.

I put the strength of nursing command in my voice. "Where's your sister, Gerald?"

He started moaning and rocking back and forth, as much as he could with Cormac's grip on his arms and Father Fraser practically sitting on him.

"Where is Cherie now?"

He spoke so low, I could barely make out the words. "She's sleeping. Sleeping forever with the fairies. Dancing under the moonlight. No one can ever wake her."

So, she must be dead. Brian had killed her. Where had he hidden her body?

"Where is she sleeping, Gerald? Give us the story. We must find her."

With more purpose than I'd yet seen on him, he looked north. Toward the bog.

Fantastic. I wanted nothing to do with that bog ever again, but we'd have to go searching for her. Maybe not at night, though.

When they eventually arrived, Gerald was considerably subdued.

I shared what Gerald had said with Adanna and Gard McCarthy. He didn't seem quite so exasperated with me now.

Imagine that.

He took notes carefully and asked questions for clarification. "Dancing with the fairies, you said?"

"Sleeping forever with the fairies. Dancing under the moonlight. Was that just mad ramblings, or is there some hidden meaning there?"

Adanna tapped her chin and looked toward the bog. "Sleeping with the fairies. That's what they used to call it when someone was given in sacrifice."

That made my blood turn cold. "Sacrifice? They still do that here?"

She shook her head with a little laugh. "No, no, I mean back in ancient times. Sleeping with the fairies meant someone had been taken to the standing stones and given in sacrifice. Sometimes, the victim volunteered. Sometimes, they were criminals. Sometimes, they were even kings."

I didn't care *who* they were. I cared *where* they were. "There are standing stones in the bog?"

Adanna and McCarthy exchanged looks, and the Gard said, "There are. Not easy to get to. We'd have to wait for daylight."

"But what if she's still alive? Out there, injured and unable to get to help?"

He stared at me, pity coloring his expression. "I highly doubt she's still alive, but you do have a fair point. I'll organize a sweep."

The Gard turned away and started speaking into his radio, calling for help from surrounding districts to conduct a manhunt.

I turned to Adanna and asked in a low tone, "Why didn't he call in help before?"

She shot a glance toward her husband, but he wasn't paying any attention to us. "He doesn't like admitting he needs help. And I don't think he believed you before."

Well, his distrust of me might hurt or kill someone now, if Cherie was still alive. I stared along the shore, silently urging her to just come out of the woods and stumble toward us. That would make any manhunt unnecessary and maybe, just maybe, assuage some of my guilt.

But she didn't. Cherie was somewhere out there, and it was my fault, at least partially. If I hadn't pushed McCarthy, no one would have gone searching for her.

The wind blew in from the ocean, and goosebumps rose on my arms. I rubbed them, but that didn't do much to warm me.

The Gard finished his conversation on the radio and turned to us. "It'll be about an hour before anyone comes. I think we should all get something to eat and warm up before heading out."

Adanna took his arm. "That sounds like a grand idea."

We all shuffled back to Cormac's pub, where he beckoned me into the kitchen. "Can you help me make soup?"

I grimaced. "I'm afraid I'm pretty useless in the kitchen, but if you're looking for unskilled labor, sure. Hey, do you have a charge cord for my phone? It's deader than…" I paused, "uh, deader than a doornail."

He let out a chuckle, and he seemed almost human. He rummaged through a drawer and handed me a white cord, pointing to a plug on the wall. "So, you do have some flaws! I can use the extra pair of hands."

His kitchen was glitzy. That's the only word for it. Everything looked state of the art, and this room was easily three times the size of the little space off my pub. Double stainless-steel sinks, a toaster with digital settings, a darned expresso machine… he could open his own café just with the kitchen.

Cormac set me to washing the vegetables while he chopped chicken and sauteed it in a pan in spices. Then, he started chopping the veg while I filled the enormous soup pot with water.

He grabbed a jar of something from the refrigerator, the largest I'd yet seen in Ireland. "Dump this whole thing into the water, and turn the burner on high, will you?"

I stared at the label. Some sort of chicken bouillon paste. I took a deep sniff and almost sneezed from the concentrated aroma. I dumped it in as he bade and stirred it. Slowly, it dissolved, leaving swirls of oily flavor trails.

I was almost mesmerized by the patterns. I must be sleepier than I realized. It was, after all, well past midnight by now. I realized I hadn't eaten in, what, ten hours? I'd earned my light-headedness.

A burst of laughter came from the main pub, and I frowned. How could they be happy while someone might be out in the bog, hurt or dying? But then I realized from my training that people in highly stressful situations sometimes needed ridiculousness as a relief valve. Especially when someone's life was at stake.

Cormac glanced over my shoulder. "Grand, toss in the veg now, and let that simmer for about twenty minutes."

"Just twenty minutes? Ar… my ex-husband would take hours to make soup."

He gave a shrug. "We don't have hours, do we? It's grand, like. It doesn't need to be gourmet. All it needs is to be hot and filling."

"That's fair."

As I continued stirring, something crawled on the back of my neck. I rubbed at it, then realized Cormac was staring at me. "What?"

"You aren't what I expected, lass."

With a raised eyebrow, I asked, "Oh? What did you expect, then?"

The older man let out a snort. "Something between a younger version of Saoirse and a money-hungry loud American tourist. You've pretty much kept yourself to yourself since you've been here."

"I haven't had much time to do anything else. Especially with strange men dying in my shed."

He stared at me for several more moments before letting out a bark of laughter. "You know? You might not be so bad, after all. Mind you," he shook a finger at me, "I still don't want you re-opening that pub. But it's just possible you won't make a total dog's dinner out of it."

I furrowed my brow. "Is that why you warned me off doing that? You were worried I'd… uh… Americanize it? I thought you were worried about the competition?"

"Ha! Have you not seen this place of an evening? It's too crowded as it is, with more wanting to get inside. We need more than one pub in this village, even during the off season. I just didn't want the other pub to be some plastic paddy tourist trap."

I gave him the first genuine smile I'd yet offered him. "Neither do I."

He stuck out a hand. "Shake on it, then?"

We shook on it.

By the time the soup was done, and everyone had shoveled down at least one bowlful, the reinforcements from the surrounding area had arrived. McCarthy organized us in groups again.

He skipped me.

"Wait, which group am I in?"

Gard McCarthy scowled at me. "You? We only need experienced folks now. You've done your part."

I crossed my arms. "Absolutely not. I am part of this now. You can't deny me this chance to find Cherie and get her home safe."

"I can and I will."

Adanna came up to her husband. "She'll be fine, Dónal. Besides, she's a nurse. If the girl is hurt, having someone with medical training on hand will be helpful. You're well aware that I won't go into the bog at night."

He growled again. "I'm not trusting an O'Shea, Adanna! You know why."

I stared at Adanna and wondered what the story was but didn't have time to delve. The Gard shot a look toward me that should have struck me dead, then nodded to two men from Schull I hadn't met. I was so tired that I barely caught their names. I think they were both named Tim but wasn't sure of anything at this point.

Perhaps staying out of the search was the better part of wisdom, but I had already made my stand and I couldn't back out now.

However, I was more than happy to let Tim and Tim take the lead. The eastern sky glowed with false dawn, and I was looking forward to daylight, especially out in the bog. Again, I wondered why Adanna was so wary of it. I'd have to ask her about her fear, but not tonight. All I wanted to do tonight was sleep in a warm bed.

My fatigue made everything blurred. The crunching of our feet on rocks, or the slurping of mud. Morning birds waking from their slumber and making their first tentative songs. The stillness of the pre-dawn shattered by people trampling through vegetation or calling out Cherie's name.

My feet were freezing, as they'd gotten wet several times. Even with the coat Seán insisted I wear, the cold sent shuddering chills through my bones. We trod on and on. Soon, I was just following the depressions in the mushy ground left by my teammates. Cold and wet and dark and exhausted. One foot in front of the other.

I paused to catch my breath, looked up, and they were gone.

I turned in a circle, looking for my teammates, listening to the silence. I couldn't even hear anyone else. How had I gotten so isolated so quickly?

Thoughts of being transported to Fairy flashed through my mind, but that was ridiculous. Besides, I was still cold and tired and miserable. Wasn't Fairy supposed to be some sort of paradise?

After a glance toward the sky to judge east, I took a tentative step south. That's where the shore should be. If I could get to the beach, I could make it safely back to civilization. I didn't even know how big the bogland was, but it was big enough to get lost in.

I circled large rocks, hummocks of vegetation, and mirror-still pools of dark water. Stepping over marsh bushes, skirting boggy ground. Then, I caught the whiff of seawater and began to walk faster. My sense of responsibility was fading as my fatigue grew.

My forward progress was halted when I couldn't lift my back foot. Confused, I looked down, and tried again, but it was stuck. *Sheep nuggets!* I tried to pull my foot out with my hands, but it was well stuck. Now the other foot was mired, as well.

What if I couldn't get out? What if I remained here forever? Images of bog bodies, buried in the muck for thousands of years, did not calm my racing heart in the slightest.

I called out, "Hello! Hello, is anyone there?"

I shone my flashlight upward, but the mist was no longer close enough to make a spotlight visible. "Hello? I need help!"

A voice answered. "Coming!" And then another with the same answer.

Rustling came from both sides, and in a moment, Cormac emerged on the left, and Seán on the right. They stared at each other for a moment, and then both reached for one of my arms.

"Hey! I'm not a wishbone!"

Sean said, "Here, I'll stand in front of you. Wrap your arms around my neck, and I'll bend forward. That should get you out."

Cormac shook his head. "That won't work, ya bleedin' mog! Grab her by the knees and lift!"

"That could break her legs!"

Instead of helping me out, they stood about a foot apart, glaring daggers at each other. Pride oozed out of each of them.

"Will you stop with the testosterone poisoning? Just get me out, first. Then you can argue about who is the manliest, right?"

Sean broke their locked gazes first, and stood in front of me. I grabbed his neck and locked my hands. He grunted and leaned forward. The mud sucked and grabbed at my feet, but slowly, slowly, they came free.

Rather than putting me down again right away, Seán carried me over his back in a fireman's carry until we got to solid ground. Once he lowered me, I stumbled. I had seriously overestimated my stamina even before I'd gotten lost, and now I was utterly exhausted.

As I sank to the ground, something bright caught my eye in the light of the rising sun.

Something pink.

"What's that over there?"

I pointed, and Cormac went to investigate. He came back with a bright pink jacket in his hand.

My skin crawled. "That's Cherie's, isn't it?"

Sean nodded. "Sure and she was wearing that when she was arguing with your man on the beach."

"And I found her scarf there, too. She might be near here."

Cormac took out his walkie-talkie, and shared that discovery with the rest of the searchers.

In about twenty minutes, others began arriving, and combing the area. I was too tired to help them, but didn't want to leave. Not yet. Not until Cherie had been found. I had just about lost hope that she'd be found alive, but there was still a sliver left, somewhere in the back of my mind.

Someone shouted, "I think she's here!" and my heart leapt.

CHAPTER TWENTY

Voices clamored all around me, a cacophony of sound, all muddled by my exhaustion. The bog stank of rotting vegetation and mud. The wind still howled through the ink-black night.

One voice clearly said, "No, she's not alive."

That's when I started fading out. Cherie no longer needed my help. She had been found.

I was warm, and I didn't know why. I forced my eyes open for a moment and found that I was lying back against Seán, his arms around me, keeping me warm. Then my eyelids drooped again, and the world went dark.

Then, I was walking. How was I walking if I wasn't even awake? But Cormac and Seán were helping me, and then Adanna took my arm. We walked forever. Well, it felt like forever, even in the morning light. The world seemed skewed. Male voices heralded that group of kids strolling past. I roused myself enough to give them a smile and a jaunty wave. I felt drunk, then faded out again.

When I finally roused, I was back in my house, in my comfy chair. When had it stopped being Gran's house? This would always be Gran's house, but perhaps it was now mine, as well.

Silverware clinked. Someone was in the kitchen. Water was being poured. I could smell something warm and soothing. They were making tea.

But I didn't want tea. I wanted sleep. In fact, I was pretty sure that I needed to sleep for a week. Adanna came in and handed me a steaming mug with a bee on it. It wasn't one of mine. Had Gran also collected bees?

"Now, drink it all. I know you want to go to bed, but you need this first. You're about frozen, and this will warm up your insides.

I did as my doctor bade me to do, though I grimaced at the bitter tea. No milk or sugar. Just hot liquid. She'd been right, I needed the warmth.

Once I was finished, she pulled me upstairs, helped me change into my pajamas, and tucked me in. I was beyond being embarrassed. Besides, she was a friend now, wasn't she? No need to be embarrassed in front of friends.

Did I go to sleep? I don't remember anything after that, except Faelan lying on my stomach, purring like an outboard motor. Soothing. Relaxing.

It seemed like an eternity before I emerged from slumber, warm sunlight streaming through the window on my face. Faelan was on my chest, whether still there from the night or again, I wasn't certain. A faint music played in the back of my mind, that almost-familiar tune. My Gran's voice echoed in my head. *Well done,* mo chroi. *You've made me proud.*

This wasn't anything out loud, but like an echo of a memory. Then the music went away, and I woke fully.

My bladder made getting up more urgent. I shoved the cat off and stumbled toward the bathroom, my legs achy from last night's activities. I noticed the pile of muddy clothing next to the hamper and grimaced. I'd have to do a wash soon, as I didn't have much of a wardrobe any longer. I'd gotten rid of so many things before I moved to Ireland.

As I got ready for the day, I reflected upon that move, and if I was still happy with my decision. Now that I was away from Armand, my old boss, and that toxic environment, I was stronger. I had more confidence in myself, and I no longer felt like I needed to run away from everything.

I might be able to take care of myself now, without anyone else's help. Well, with the help of the community, but not that of an abusive husband, at the very least.

I might even finally have the mental energy to crack open one of Gran's crossword puzzle books.

Faelan shoved into my legs. "Yes, and the help of a rude fairy cat, too."

And my help, of course.

I halted in the midst of sorting my laundry. There was that music again, but I was fully awake now. I could no longer write it off as the scrap of a dream. "Gran?"

Of course. Who else would it be?

I had no answer to that. "You're still here? Are you… are you a ghost?"

Laughter filled my mind. *No, nothing like that. But now that you've passed the first test, I'm here if and when you need me. I'll help as much as I can. Sometimes I can only help through Faelan, but rest assured, we're on your team. You will be able to do good things here.*

"Well, at least I was able to help find the killer. Despite his attempts to make it look supernatural, there was a logical explanation to the Dearg-Due."

Oh, but there was *a Dearg-Due. Who do you think answered his howls in the night? Cherie possessed Gerald to enact her vengeance, though he might not have understood that.*

I sat up straight, my heart pounding. "Wait, so the Dearg-Due *is* real? Is she going to kill again?"

No, no, she did what she came to do, and is resting now. However, now that one of the Fair Folk has been roused, others will come forth. And they will seek you out, I'm afraid.

Dumping the rest of my ripped, muddy clothes on the floor, I stopped again. "Others?"

The hills of Ireland are deep with the Fair Folk, mo chroi. *You have the powers, and the duty, to keep them from wreaking too much mischief. And the keys.*

That made goosebumps rise on my arms. "The keys? You mean the iron ring? What are they for?"

You shall discover that in due time.

"And Adanna? She seems to know a lot about the fairies, too."

She's got her own powers, to be sure. But your paths are not the same.

Everything was crowding in on me, and the urge to run grew strong. "But what if I don't want to do all this? What if I just want a peaceful life?"

I'm afraid that's not an option, dear. It's a burden our family has always held. You'll have our help, and others. You'll know them when you see them.

I didn't want all this. Danger was never something I'd sought out. I wasn't one of those who loved diving out of perfectly good airplanes or bungee jumped off bridges. I didn't even like sports like skiing. "But… but what am I supposed to do?"

You will find out. The first thing you must do is finish reading my diary. There are many clues in there to help you arm yourself.

I definitely didn't like the sound of that. Still, if that was the price of living in this lovely village, in my Gran's pub, I supposed the price was worth it. I looked forward to being part of a real community for the first time in my life.

A bell rang in the distance. Oh, no! Today was Sunday, wasn't it? I'd promised Father Fraser I'd go to Mass.

Well, after the events of last night, he should be able to forgive me for skipping this morning. I hoped.

Staring out of the little window in the laundry room, a bee flew by, meandering in lazy circles. I remembered seeing that bee at the castle, back when I first arrived in Ireland. Seeing it land on the rusty iron lock.

My future would be full of fairy creatures, yes, but also abundance and a community. I was welcomed here, and this could be my real home.

Besides, running away again wouldn't do me any good.

Reimagining her life isn't going as planned. When a renovation turns into a crime scene, can she get to the bottom of a nightmare turned murder?

Start reading ***Whispers, Whiskey, and Wishes*** for a shot in the dark today!

Books2read.com/Whispers-Whiskey-and-Wishes

THANK YOU!

Thank you so much for enjoying ***Bogs, Brews, and Banshees.*** If you've enjoyed the story, please consider leaving a review to help others discover Skye's adventures!

If you'd like to get updates, sneak previews, sales, and **FREE STUFF**, please sign up for my newsletter.
www.GreenDragonArtist.com

See all the books available
through Green Dragon Publishing at
www.GreenDragonArtist.com/Books

DEDICATION

For anyone who has ached to start a new life, this book is for you. It's a scary thing, to leave everything behind. To start anew and rebuild each aspect of yourself. But sometimes, it's the only thing left to do.

ACKNOWLEDGEMENTS

I have such a wonderful group of friends, both authors and readers, who have helped me with this book. The first book in a new genre is always a frightening gamble, but I've had lots of support and I appreciate everyone who has helped me.

PRONUNCIATION GUIDE AND GLOSSARY

Amádan – [ah-mah-DAWN] foolish person.
Ballybás – [bah-lee-BAWS] town of the dead.
Ban sídhe – [bahn SHEE] a fairy who wails for the dead of a particular family.
Cat sídhe – [kat SHEE] a fairy cat.
Cormac – [KOHR-mick]
Cú Chulainn – [koo-HOO-linn] an ancient Irish hero.
Dearg-Due – [DAH-rugh DOO-ah] a vengeful Irish spirit who steals blood.
Dia duit – [JEE-ah GWICH] Hello (literally, God be with you).
Fear Dearg – [FAR DAH-rugh] mischievous Irish fairy (literally, red man).
Máiréad – [MY-rid]
Mo chroí – [muh CROY] my heart.
Na dean magadh fum – [nah den MAGgah foom] "Do not mock me."
Pádraig – [POH-rig]
Saoirse – [SEER-shah] Freedom.
Sétanta – [sheh-TAWN-the] an ancient Irish hero.
Slainte – [SLAWN-chah] Good luck.
Sluagh Sídhe – [SLOO-ah SHEE] fairies who steal dying souls.

ABOUT THE AUTHOR

Christy Nicholas writes under several pen names, including Rowan Dillon, C.N. Jackson, and Emeline Rhys. She's an author, artist, and accountant. After she failed to become an airline pilot, she quit her ceaseless pursuit of careers that began with the letter 'A' and decided to concentrate on her writing. Since she has Project Completion Compulsion, she is one of the few authors with no unfinished novels.

Christy has her hands in many crafts, including digital art, beaded jewelry, writing, and photography. In real life, she's a CPA, but having grown up with art all around her (her mother, grandmother, and great-grandmother are/were all artists), it sort of infected her, as it were. She wants to expose the incredible beauty in this world, hidden beneath the everyday grime of familiarity and habit, and share it with others. She uses characters out of time and places infused with magic and myth, writing magical realism stories in both historical fantasy and time travel flavors.

Social Media Links:

Blog: www.GreenDragonArtist.net
Website: www.GreenDragonArtist.com
Facebook: www.facebook.com/greendragonauthor
Instagram: www.instagram.com/greendragonartist9
TikTok: www.tiktok.com/@greendragonauthor

Printed in the USA
CPSIA information can be obtained
at www.ICGtesting.com
LVHW091611270624
784159LV00007B/139

9 798869 177858